The
Princess

A FAIRY TALE

The Princess

A Fairy Tale

MICHAEL CRISTIAN

ARPress
45 Dan Road Suite 5
Canton MA 02021

Hotline: 1(800) 220-7660
Fax: 1(855) 752-6001

Ordering Information:
Quantity sales. Special discounts are available on quantity purchases by corporations, associations, and others. For details, contact the publisher at the address above.

Printed in the United States of America.

ISBN-13:   Paperback   978-8-89389-715-9
           eBook   978-8-89389-716-6

Library of Congress Control Number: 2024922137

For my mother, Anastacia
The princess of all mothers, humble of heart

This is a Fairy Tale!

Welcome to the Magical and Mystical
Land of the Princess!

A ship sets anchor somewhere off the coast in northern Spain (Hispana). It arrived from a long voyage to the land of Tenoc (Mexico). A row boat comes to shore. A gentleman standing next to a carriage awaits.

"It's an honor to see you again, Highness."

"Thank you Marcos. How is father?"

"All is well, highness. He awaits your arrival."

She turns and smiles.

The Princess: "I'm glad to hear it."

The princess climbs onto the horse-drawn carriage.

The Princess: "Come on Xitl, to the palace we go!"

Xitl: "Yes, my princess. If I can just get on this strange… boat?"

The princess laughs.

The Princess: "It's a carriage Xitl! And these are called horses."

Xitl: "Beautiful creatures."

They ride off into the forest. Soon they arrive at San Juan Castle.

GUARD: "IT'S THE PRINCESS! OPEN THE GATES!"

Gates open. Princess Malina and her Aztec servant and friend Xitl walk in. It is a long hallway/tunnel. There are royal palace guards on both sides. They bow their heads in respect as the princess walks by.

Xitl: "Wow, my princess! You must feel very honored and important to have such treatment and glory!"

Malina: "I was born to this Xitl. Nothing more, I didn't earn it."

Xitl looks at his princess.

Xitl: "But you must appreciate all this!"

Malina: "Yes, of course I do. I'm me. I'm here. Someday, if I am ever queen, I will make it my mission to earn the respect and obedience of my people and keep it."

Xitl: "What do you mean if? You will be queen someday, my princess! The entire kingdom of Hispana will be yours, just wait and see."

Princess Malina looks at Xitl and smiles delightfully.

Malina: "Oh Xitl, I like you. You make me feel good and happy. Don't ever change. Keep amusing me."

Xitl: "Highness, I am not here to amuse you. I am here to protect you."

Malina: "Ha, ha, ha! I think I'm the one who's been doing all the protecting."

Xitl frowns.

Xitl: "I made a promise to your mother, my queen."

Malina: "I miss her already."

Xitl: "Please my princess, don't do that. You'll make me cry."

Malina sighs.

Malina: "You men are so weak."

Xitl: "Weak? You're the one who wants to shed tears."

Malina: "That's why women are the stronger. We let go, holding nothing back. Men think they are strong by holding back their emotions and true feelings. It only weakens them."

Xitl: "I'm sorry, my princess. I do not share your views. I am Xitl, Aztec warrior. I cannot show weakness through tears. I would ruin my entire lineage of noble blood."

Malina: "Still following the teachings of Quetzalcoatl?"

Xitl: "And why not? He is the strongest and wisest of all the gods!"

Malina: "I doubt that."

Xitl: "You think so? Oh yes, of course. You follow the way of the ancient carpenter. A simple man whom they say walked on water."

Malina: "I'm impressed Xitl. How did you learn of my God?"

Xitl: "Uh, these teachers. Men who travel the world teaching the ways of the carpenter. Our nobles let them into the city to speak. I listened to their rants."

Malina: "Rants?"

The princess laughed.

Xitl: "Yes. Well, quite a story about this man."

Malina: "But you chose not to follow?"

Xitl: "I don't understand the way of the carpenter. They say he is the only god in the world with great power and yet, he allowed himself to be killed for a greater purpose. I just don't understand why a god would do that. It only shows weakness, great weakness. It shows he is no god at all, only a mortal man."

Malina: "Ah, but the carpenter resurrected and came back to life to show the world the full glory of God!"

Xitl groaned and stared at Malina. Malina smiled happily.

Malina: "Oh, Xitl. I wish I had the wise words of the teachers to persuade you. But if they couldn't do it, then how will I? I can only pray for you."

Xitl: "No need, my princess. I am strong and brave. Someday, Quetzalcoatl will return and when he does, I will reign with him in his kingdom forever."

Malina: "Hmm, sounds similar to my beliefs."

Xitl: "My princess, do not be offended. But my belief is men are stronger than females."

Malina: "No."

Xitl: "No? Give me one good reason why you don't think so."

Malina: "Because men are made out of dirt, ashes. Women are made out of solid bone."

Xitl: "What? What do you mean? Is this a riddle?"

Malina: "Nevermind."

Xitl: "I'm not made out of dirt."

Malina again laughed and continued onward.

Xitl: "Highness, I'm not made out of dirt! Wait for me!"

Inside the royal palace are numerous guests: representatives of the court, man-guards stood at attention, and joy and laughter all around. The king's chancellor approached him with news.

Chancellor: "Your majesty? Sire, we've just received word that her highness Princess Ma..."

(Palace Music Plays)

(A royal guard pounds the palace floor with the bottom end of his high spear.)

Palace Announcer: "The princess of Aragon! Her majesty, Princess Malina de Zaragoza!"

Everyone applauds and bows in respect for their princess. The king rises from his decorated throne. He slightly waves his hand. Almost immediately, silence fills the palace hall.

Palace Announcer: "The king of Hispana! His majesty, King Esteban de Zaragoza!"

The king looks at his daughter. Malina looks back. He smiles and opens his arms.

Malina runs and embraces her father. Everyone cheers.

King Esteban: "Malinali! My Malinali! You're home!"

Malina: "Oh father, I've missed you so."

King Esteban: "How was your journey?"

Malina: "It was wonderful father!"

King Esteban: "You must be very tired."

Malina: "Yes I am. It's good to be home father."

King Esteban: "You've brought a friend?"

Xitl raises his fist in the air and bows his head in greeting to the king.

Malina: "Father, this is my good friend, Xitl. We met in the valley of Xochimilco."

King Esteban: "Ah yes. The flower land, millions upon millions upon millions of beautiful flowers. A king can truly rest in peace surrounded in its bed."

Xitl: "Oh king, I am honored to meet you finally. It is a privilege to serve Princess Malina."

King Esteban: "I thank you."

Xitl: "I will defend her with my life! I am Aztec! Warrior. Conqueror. My teacher was Fallen Eagle. As Malina's one true protector, I..."

Malina: "Xitl?"

Xitl: "Yes, my princess?"

Malina: "He gets the idea."

Xitl frowns.

Malina: "Anyway father. I'm home now. I've been away these many months and now I just want to spend time with you."

King Esteban: "How is your mother?"

Malina: "She's fine. She misses you. She always talks about you."

King Esteban: "And I miss her, so very much. You know why I sent her away. To protect her. To keep her safe."

Malina looks at her father.

Malina: "Yes, I know the reasons all too well."

The king looks at Malina. How he loved his daughter so.

Malina: "The Great War is coming, I know."

King Esteban: "Come, come, we'll have no talk of war this day. Tonight, we shall celebrate my daughter's return! The princess has come home!"

[HOORAY! HOORAY! HOORAY!]

All in the palace cheer and shout happily. Princess Malina was home!

The royal celebration took place in the banquet hall of the castle. Everything was beautifully decorated and very elaborate. Court jesters jumped and leaped about, dancing and flipping in the air. Servants walked around tending and serving food and drinks to all at court.

"Hurry Mother! We're late as it is!"

"Silence child. There's plenty of time. Get back here and make up your face."

"It's a masquerade ball Mother, no need."

"Just do it Simona."

Simona closed the curtain window and sat next to her mother Sonia.

Simona: "We're always having celebrations and parties. Why is this so different?"

Sonia: "Didn't you hear? The princess has returned back from her mother's native country."

Simona: "She's so lucky, Malina. Must be nice to be a princess of two nations."

Sonia: "Indeed, child."

Simona stared at herself in the large mirror.

Simona: "I want to be a princess, Mother."

Sonia looked at her daughter. She smirked.

Sonia: "Do you? And why is that my dear?"

Simona: "I just do is all. I want servants to kneel before me and to serve my every bidding whenever I want. But instead, I'm a servant myself and sadly so are you, Mother. It's not fair!"

Sonia: "What if I was to tell you that you already are a princess, my child?"

Simona stared abruptly at her mother, strikingly surprised.

Simona: "What do you mean?"

Sonia: "It's just a simple question, Simona."

Simona: "No, it isn't, Mother. It's a strong and accusatory statement."

Sonia laughed while powdering her face.

Sonia: "Hardly accusatory, child."

Simona: "I ask you again, Mother. What do you mean if I was already a princess?"

Sonia turned to her daughter.

Sonia: "Simona, you are the bastard child of King Esteban."

Simona's jaw dropped in complete awe.

Simona: "What Mother?"

Sonia: "It's the truth, my dear child. You are the king's daughter, his second-born."

Simona could not believe what she just heard from her mother's lips! She tried to gasp for air.

Sonia: "Darling? Are you alright? Breathe, just breathe."

Sonia took hold of Simona and helped her stand. Simona's face dissolved into tears.

An involuntary cry wrenched from her throat.

Simona: "I'm a princess? I... I'm a p... I'm a princess!"

Sonia: "There now child. Sit, sit."

Simona: "How could you not tell me, Mother? Why?"

Sonia: "Because I was afraid, you know the penalty for adultery. Oh yes, nothing ever happens to the man. But for the women, she is either cast out or put to death! And here in this realm, the penalty is death by hanging!"

Simona cried. Sonia hugged her daughter tightly.

Sonia: "I kept the truth from you to protect you! To protect us. Now listen to me and listen good."

Simona looked at her mother.

Sonia: "Fifteen years ago, I was sent here from another realm. I was a server in the king's court. He took a liking to me and fancied me. The queen suspected and always eyed me with distaste. She knew, but what would she achieve by saying anything?"

Simona: "Does she know about me?"

Sonia: "I don't know for sure. About the affair, yes. About you? Evidently, she has never made it known. You and I are still here."

Simona: "So the king doesn't know? He doesn't know about me? That I'm his daughter?"

Sonia: "Heavens no! If he did, we'd be banned from the realm or dead. Even you child. No way would he ever allow his shame to be made public."

Simona: "So why do you tell me now?"

Sonia sighed.

Sonia: "As you know, the Great War is coming. The pagan Emirs have invaded the surrounding countries nearby, that's why the king sent the queen away. I am more comfortable with her not being here. I'm glad of it."

Sonia caressed Simona's hair.

Sonia: "And also..."

Simona: "And also?"

Sonia: "The king is dying."

Simona's eyes widened with disbelief.

Simona: "What? The king...my father is dying? How?"

Sonia: "He's been sick for some time now, an unknown sickness. His physicians are still unsure of what it is and how to treat it. I suspect old age, but what do I know."

Simona: "What do you plan to do mother? Are you going to tell him now?"

Sonia: "Now that the queen is gone and with everything happening, I feel the time may be right for the truth to be finally exposed."

Simona: "And what of Princess Malina? My... sister?"

Sonia: "What about her?"

Simona: "Well, doesn't she deserve to know also?"

Sonia: "What Malina doesn't know won't hurt her. She will never know. At least not now while her father lives."

Simona: "But why not, mother?"

Sonia looked at her daughter boldly.

Sonia: "Because child..."

Simona gasped.

Simona: "Mother? No, I..."

Sonia: "Look at me! You are the king's daughter. You're a princess and you will have your rightful place in his kingdom. You will be the princess of Aragon! You are full-blooded Spana! No way will I let that half-breed 'mestizan' slut steal away your birthright!"

Simona stared hard at her mother. Sonia grinned.

Sonia: "Now, doesn't that sound awfully pleasant?"

Simona slowly smiled.

Sonia: "Ah! She's happy? Good. Now, go and get yourself ready. You must be cheerful and lovely like the beautiful princess that you are!"

Simona: "Yes, mother."

Sonia: "And remember, not a word of this to anyone."

Simona nodded.

Simona: "Mother?"

Sonia: "Yes dear?"

Simona: "How do you know of the king's health? Who told you?"

Sonia looked at Simona.

Sonia: "Well, my dear. The king is not dead yet. He still fancies me, you know."

Simona laughed.

Simona: "Mother! You are a conniving little bitch, aren't you? Ha, ha, ha!"

Sonia: "Well, the ripples of water all come from the same drop. Do they not my dear?"

Simona smiled happily and danced joyfully.

Simona: "Hurry Mother, we must put on our masks!"

Sonia: "Mine is here. Yours is on top of the dresser."

Simona: "Oh, I wasn't referring to our masks, Mother dearest."

Sonia: "No?"

Simona: "I was referring to our... masks!"

Sonia turned to her daughter in surprise.

Sonia: "And I thought I was the only conniving little bitch in the palace!"

Simona and Sonia looked at each other in the mirror and laughed. They continued putting on their make-up. They would join the others in the banquet hall soon enough.

It was a joyous occasion. The king invited nobles and lords throughout the realm. Dignitaries came and paid respect to the young princess. Maidens brought Malina gifts. The princess was very happy. She was grateful to everyone. But not everyone was at the banquet. Malina thought of her love, Alberto. He was a simple young man who came from a simple and poor family. Alberto was an apprentice of a skilled blacksmith and sword-maker. In time, Alberto would become skilled enough to go off on his own. But like most young men growing up, he always dreamed of becoming a noble knight in the king's service. So young Alberto joined and that's how he met the young and lovely princess. The two almost immediately fell in love at first glance.

However, a beautiful princess always has other suitors who also want to win her heart. This caused trouble for the "in love" pair. Even though Malina loved Alberto because she was of noble birth she had no say in the matter. It was not even up to the king himself. The matter had to be settled between two knights by way of combat!

Both knights had a choice, either by duel of swords at dawn or joust on horseback. If a knight chose the sword, he was considered brave. If a knight chose the joust, he was considered cautious. Reason being that when dueling with swords, one or the other was certain to die. Jousting was no less dangerous, but chances of survival were a lot better. Alberto was a skilled sword-maker but not a skilled swordsman, though he was a knight. With honor he chose the joust. His opponent Garcia mocked him!

Garcia: "Joust? Can not the noble knight use a sword up to his person? Surely the princess deserves a better battle and a worthier knight in the fight for her honor?"

Alberto: "Your majesty, I'm proud to be a knight in your majesty's service. However, everyone knows, including your majesty, that Garcia is the best swordsman of all the knights in Castile and I give him respect and honor. But if it pleases your majesty, I choose the joust. That is how I want to win the princess."

Garcia: "And I choose the sword! Sword-maker!"

Alberto looked at Garcia. Garcia grinned and smirked at him. Alberto then looked at his beloved Princess Malina. Malina stared back at Alberto. How she loved him so, but she was powerless to do anything to help him.

King Esteban: "Well, gentlemen. It seems we have a dilemma, an impasse. I'm afraid I have no choice but to delay the combat and ask the people to decide the outcome."

Garcia: "Sire, we could just as easily toss a coin to determine this."

Alberto: "Sire?"

King Esteban: "Yes Knight?"

Alberto: "Majesty? Could we allow the princess to decide, sire?"

Garcia chuckled at the idea.

The king looked silently at Alberto.

Garcia: "With respect to her highness sire, isn't it the rule of the kingdom that even a princess shall have no word?"

The king looked at Garcia. Garcia looked at Alberto. Alberto locked eyes with Malina.

King Esteban: "Princess Malina?"

Malina: "Yes, your majesty?"

King Esteban: "These two brave knights both want your hand in marriage. Is that not so?"

Malina shook with nervousness. She tried to calm herself.

Malina: "Yes sire, that is so."

King Esteban: "Then how would you have them resolve this, by sword or joust?"

Garcia could not believe the king was actually asking his daughter's opinion. Malina looked at Alberto. She felt a sense of hope.

Malina: "If… if it pleases your majesty, I think the combat should be not by way of swords but by way of the joust… sire."

Alberto smiled.

King Esteban: "Then by the joust it shall be."

The tournament was set, hundreds of people attended. Both knights were at the ready. Garcia and Alberto boldly looked each other down.

Announcer: "Remember caballeros, you each have three chances! Whoever touches the other first is what counts! Whether or not your lance breaks, as long as it lands upon the other's shield or armor, it is a point! Remember, this is a simple joust! If one of you are unhorsed, the other knight wins and the match is over! There will be no continuing duel on the ground floor if one or both are unhorsed! Do you understand?"

Alberto and Garcia continued staring at each other. A simple joust? No matter. The stakes were still high!

Announcer: "Caballeros! The field is yours! Adelante!"

Both knights pulled down their visor and gripped their lances tight. All were silent. Malina's heart raced uncontrollably. The king slowly raised his hand in the air and then dropped it swiftly. The challenge commenced forth. The crowd roared! Alberto and Garcia raced toward each other with great speed. To Alberto's good fortune, his lance tipped Garcia's shield first. This angered Garcia heavily.

Both knights each dropped their first lance and took hold of a new one that was set on a stand. The two faced off again and charged at each other once more. This time Garcia fared well. His lance tipped Alberto's shield forcefully. They were tied. Once more they charged. Closer and closer, the two riders met. Garcia's lance crushed upon Alberto's armor, nearly knocking Alberto off his horse! Malina quickly turned her face away in shock. How she feared for Alberto. Two points for Garcia.

Garcia: "One more point! One more point!"

Alberto tried to breathe steadily. The striking lance knocked the wind out of him. Garcia laughed. He turned and looked out at the princess. Malina turned away. She loathed Garcia.

Garcia: "Turn away, my princess, turn away. Soon you shall be mine. All mine! Ha, ha, ha!"

Alberto's friend Pedro came up to check on him.

Pedro: "Alberto, are you alright? Can you continue?"

Alberto: "I have to."

Pedro: "Alberto, he has two hits. You have one."

Alberto: "I know my friend, I'll be fine."

All Garcia needed was one more point to win the tournament and thus also win his suit for Malina's hand in marriage. Alberto's heart raced with vibrancy. Could he lose this match? Again both knights faced off looking towards one another, lance in hand. Alberto closed his visor. He kicked his heels and once more the elegantly draped horse ran in full gallop to meet the other opposing combatant. Malina's pulse throbbed vigorously. She could not look. She just could not. Closer and closer, nearer and nearer the knights engaged. Garcia readied his long lance. Malina gasped as she closed her eyes whispering her beloved knight's name.

"Alberto!"

Alberto suddenly dropped his feet from the saddled stirrups. He immediately tossed his shield, grabbed hold of the pommel with his left hand, and quickly jumped upon the saddle using it as a base to stand on. To everyone's astonishment, Alberto stood and jumped in the air as high as he could, raising his lance with his right hand, plunging downward into Garcia's shield and armor! The blow knocked Garcia completely off his horse! It was a stunning moment for all to see. Alberto himself landed on the ground hard. Malina's jaw dropped in awe. She rose up from her chair and cheered her brave knight!

Alberto won! Or had he? Nothing like this was ever done before in a jousting match. There were no rules stating that a knight could do or not do the mesmerizing act that Alberto did. Because of the confusion and uncertainty, it was declared that Alberto had not won the match nor lost either. It was declared a draw. Neither Alberto or Garcia had won Malina's hand. Malina's heart belonged to Alberto, he already knew that, but he could never marry her legally. After the match, the knights of the realm didn't know how to receive or treat Alberto. Some applauded his brave and daring act, others shunned him. Many were loyal to Garcia and therefore singled out Alberto.

After sometime, Alberto decided to leave the knighthood. He saw no further reason to stay. Alberto packed his things and moved away. Malina was saddened. She cried herself to sleep many nights thinking of him. How she loved her brave knight. She feared she would never see him again.

The festival celebration lasted all through the late hours of the night and into the early morning. Malina slowly awoke from her bed by a tiny voice inside a small glowing image! Malina smiled.

Malina: "Good morning Lila!"

Lila: "Good morning, your highness! Time to arise and be fruitful! What shall we have this glorious morning?"

Malina yawned and stretched out her arms.

Malina: "Well Lila, let's see. How about some jack-jacks with syrup and strawberries?"

Lila: "As you wish highness. Milk or juice? Let me guess, juice?"

Malina: "You guessed it!"

Lila was an Arielantis, a type of fairy with limited powers who served the royal family of Hispana. Lila waived her arms in a circular motion and before Malina's eyes appeared a small elegant table adjusted gently over her legs with the warm and delicious items she requested.

Lila: "Your majesty, breakfast is served!"

Malina: "Thank you Lila! You are always a delight!"

Lila: "Enjoy!"

With that, Lila bowed her head to the princess and mystically vanished. Malina unwrapped her napkin and took hold of her knife and fork. As she ate her meal, she suddenly remembered something.

Malina: "Oh no? Lila! Li..."

A loud scream echoed through the palace! Malina laughed uncontrollably.

Malina: "Xitl, I'm sorry! I forgot to mention that Lila would magically appear in your room! Ha, ha, ha!"

Later in the day, Malina went to see her father in his chambers.

King Esteban: "I'm glad you came home. You've brought joy and laughter once again into this house."

Malina: "I'm so glad to be home, Father. I'm happy to be here with you at your side."

King Esteban: "Much has happened while you've been away. I wish..."

Malina: "Father please, don't distress yourself."

King Esteban: "I'm happy you're here Malinali, if only for a while. There's still time for you to get away."

Malina: "Let's not worry about that now."

King Esteban smiled at his daughter.

Malina: "Mother wanted me to stay, but I didn't want to leave you."

King Esteban: "You'll never leave me, Malinali. I'll always keep you close by. However, I have a duty as king to protect my homeland and my kingdom, as does your mother hers."

Malina: "Mother will be fine. Sure, there may be one or two tribes with unrest trying to overtake the Aztec empire, but no real danger. Mostly politics, not warfare."

King Esteban: "Oh my child, how little you know. Politics is the aim of warfare. War is caused because of political men."

Malina looked at her father.

Malina: "Such as a king?"

King Esteban: "That's not fair."

Malina: "Isn't it? I'm not always naïve, Father. And I'm not as gullible as many may think. I know some of the ways of the world."

King Esteban: "A father's discontent, especially when the ways of the world concern my daughter. That is why I would feel better knowing you were safe in your mother's homeland."

Malina: "Oh father, I'm a princess, aren't I? Of course I'll always be safe. Palace guards here, royal guards there! Jaguar knights here, Eagle knights there! I'm a princess in two kingdoms! Why can't I be just me? Sometimes I just want to be me."

King Esteban: "Why do I feel I'm not the only reason you've decided to return?"

Malina glanced at her father. She sighed softly.

Malina: "I had hoped..."

King Esteban: "Yes?"

Malina: "Have you heard anything?"

King Esteban: "Not a word, just that he moved away. No one knows where."

Malina: "You knew I loved him and I still do Father."

King Esteban: "I know, child."

Malina: "Why didn't you proclaim him victory? Alberto won. He won my hand fairly."

King Esteban: "Malinali, please, we've discussed this already. What Alberto did was remarkable but unheard of. Never in the history of the joust has a knight ever attempt such a feat. The royal assembly were unsure of what to do. A knight is to remain seated upon his horse unless and only unless the other knight lances him off while he himself is required to remain seated. That is how the joust is played. Alberto violated the tradition if not the rule. I alone as king could not simply declare him victorious. It would not have been right."

Malina: "I'm sorry father. I don't mean to sound selfish or ungrateful. I just... I..."

King Esteban: "I know, my child, I know. Do not worry. Come, I'll arrange a carriage for us. Let us sight see the open country."

Malina: "Oh Father, can we go to the village markets?"

King Esteban: "You're the princess!"

Malina was overcome with joy. She hugged her father happily.

Malina: "Thank you father! Thank you! Xitl must come with me!"

King Esteban: "Yes, bring your friend. Show him around. It'll be good."

Malina: "Yes!"

Malina dashed down the hallway, yelling out Xitl's name with glee. Everyone in the palace smiled.

Xitl: "My princess? What is wrong? What is it?"

Malina swiftly caught hold of Xitl's hand.

Malina: "Come on silly! We're going to the market."

Xitl: "Uh, okay?"

The crown carriage awaited them outside with footmen and man-guards at the ready. Xitl was astonished. The crown carriage was even more beautiful than the previous carriage! Malina was overjoyed having her friend with her.

Driver: "Where do you wish to go my king?"

King Esteban: "Better to ask my daughter, Delio."

Driver: "Your highness?"

Malina: To the market. Thank you, Delio."

Delio bowed his head and drove off. The horses galloped with authority. Princess Malina, the king, and Xitl departed.

It was a beautiful day. Malina enjoyed seeing the lovely sights of the kingdom. She enjoyed spending time with her father. She especially had fun shopping in the market villages. She came across a fruit stand. An old gypsy woman in a hooded cloak greeted her.

Old Woman: "Greetings, your majesty! And what would her highness like today? I have bananas, pears, grapes, apples, and oranges. May I entice my young princess to an apple?"

Malina looked at the shiny apple. It was very tempting indeed. The old gypsy woman held the large apple up close.

Old Woman: "Tis very good my princess! Tasty indeed!"

The old woman smiled at Malina, all the while waving the apple from side to side. Malina smiled. She reached out and took hold of the large and shiny apple. Malina stared at the red fruit. She raised it above her and looked at it. The old woman stared at her. Malina slowly brought the delicious apple toward her mouth. She faced the old gypsy woman and smiled.

Malina: "Oh Ofelia, you know me already. I'm a banana girl!"

Ofelia the gypsy woman laughed happily.

Ofelia: "I had a feeling it was going to be the usual as always highness!"

Malina: "Can I have two bags?"

Ofelia: "Two bags of bananas coming right up, your majesty!"

Malina smiled happily. Ofelia put the bananas in the two bags. Malina gave Ofelia two pesetas for the order.

Ofelia: "Here you are my princess, have a wonderful day."

Malina: "Thank you Ofelia, until next time."

Ofelia bowed her head in respect. Malina gave her a hug and left. She met up with her father the king and her Aztec friend Xitl. The three continued onward through the crowded market with the king's man-guards following close behind.

Deep within the caves of the dark Atlas Mountains, a meeting is taking place. The Zor of Moroc speaks before his army.

Zor Of Moroc: "Armies of Moroc, heed my words! The time has come to spread the prophecies of the true faith! Praise be to the One! Protector and Guardian of all Moroc! I have heard him. We will spread his word like an unending inferno. We begin with our enemies in the North! The kingdom of Hispana stands in our way. Long have we been sworn enemies. Long have we fought. The time has come to end our conflict once and for all!"

All the armies cheered.

Zor: "Tomorrow night, we set sail for Hispana! In darkness we will begin and in darkness we will end!"

The army of Moroc cheered and applauded their leader. The nations of Hispana and Moroc have been at war for religious differences. This would be the greatest war of all, to determine religious freedom and human supremacy! While the cheering and roaring continued, two dark voices sounded in the blackness of the deep caves above. Their eyes glowed bright red.

["Did you hear that Milagro?"]

["I (puff!) sure did Antonio. What are we gonna do? We have no power here in this realm. (puft!) Only in our homeland."]

Antonio: ["I know. Our powers don't last long in another land. I can feel myself growing weak."]

Milagro: ["This looks bad."]

Antonio: ["We better get back and report everything we heard to the Don."]

Milagro: ["Hey, you think he'll reward us this time?"]

Antonio: ["Doesn't he always?"]

Milagro: ["Hmm. (puff!) I don't remember."]

Antonio: ["Come on, let's go."]

Both Antonio and Milagro slowly crept backwards into the deep hollow caverns of the high mountains.

The Zor of Moroc enters a secret chamber. A dark figure awaits from afar, she is an old woman dressed in a hooded cloak. The Zor looks toward her. The Witch of Sevi stands by the river of blood.

Witch: "Your army sounds optimistic, my lord."

Zor: "My soldiers are warriors of the true faith and would die for the One. The way of the carpenter is dead, the One will lead us to victory once and for all!"

The witch laughs.

Witch: "Are you so sure?"

Zor: "Why do you ask, mistress? Do you doubt the power of the One?"

Witch: "Let's just say I do not doubt the power of evil."

The Zor looks at her curiously.

Witch: "I have seen the power of the promised one, we must not underestimate it, especially now."

Zor: "Why now?"

The Witch of Sevi kneels and stares deeply into the river of blood. Her eyes clench and twitch.

Witch: "She has returned. She is stronger than before and she is very wise."

Zor: "What do you see? Whom do you speak of?"

Witch: "Her, you fool, her!"

The Zor looks into the river of blood.

Zor: "A girl? A young girl? And how is she a threat to us?"

Witch: "Because you fool, her god is with her. You must destroy her."

Zor: "Who is she mistress?"

Witch: "The princess of Aragon, the maiden of Tenoc."

Zor: "What is her name?"

Witch: "Her Tenician name is Malinali. Her Spanian name is Malina."

Zor: "Aztec mother? Spanian father?"

Witch: "Yes, the mestizan princess has returned and we must be cautious. She must not ascend to the throne."

Zor: "We sail for Hispana tomorrow night. Things are underway which cannot be stopped. Not even her god can help her."

Witch: "I'll be watching, make your conquest prevail."

Zor: "It shall, I have my greatest commander leading them."

Witch: "And that is?"

Zor: "Tarak, my noble warrior."

Witch: "Whatever your conquests, just make sure she dies."

The Zor bowed his head to the Witch of Sevi and left.

Meanwhile, in the night sky, two fire-breathing dragons are flying, piercing the rumbling clouds of the air, soaring back to Hispana.

Milagro: ["I don't know Antonio. I think this time (puff!) all of Hispana is in danger."]

Antonio: ["I think you're right Milagro. The armies of Moroc have multiplied. They've gotten stronger, much stronger."]

Milagro: ["The Don will know what to do."]

Antonio: ["Let us hope so, my good friend. The entire kingdom depends on it. We don't have much time."]

Milagro: ["We must protect the princess! (puff!)"]

Antonio: ["We will, don't worry."]

The dark sky rumbled as the two Spano dragons flew, cutting across through the horizon. They would soon reach the kingdom of Hispana.

In the small village of Villalobos, a celebration for a wedding is taking place.

Everyone was happy and joyful.

Minister: "May you two enjoy a long and happy life together. May Christ grant you the joy of many children. To the bride and groom!"

Everyone cheered. As the party continued, a messenger came and asked the host for a certain person. The host pointed at a certain direction. The messenger followed.

Messenger: "Senor Gali?"

An old man turned.

Gali: "Yes?"

Messenger: "I was ordered to give this to you personally."

Gali: "Thank you, you may go."

Messenger: "Sir."

The messenger departed. Gali broke the seal and opened the letter.

The letter read:

> *Don Gali,*
>
> *I have just returned home from my mother's homeland of Tenoc. My father was so overwhelmed with happiness of my return that he announced a celebrational feast in my honor that very night. I do most heartily regret not having the proper timing of inviting you.*
>
> *Be that as it may, I cordially invite you to dine with us tomorrow evening. I eagerly anticipate your arrival. The royal palace of San Juan awaits you!*
>
> *Blessings upon you, Don Gali.*
>
> *Sincerely,*
> *Malinali 'The Princess'*

The old man smiled.

Gali: "An invitation? How thoughtful."

Gali, the Don of Villalobos, would be happy to attend the royal feast.

The next night was the royal dinner. Not as festive as the royal banquet like before, but still joyous and cheerful just the same. Princess Malina looked at herself in a long mirror. One of the servants brushed her beautiful black hair.

Malina: "I wish Alberto was here. Now when I need him most, he's away, far away. My dear love…"

Servant: "I'm sorry, your highness. May I ask, any idea of where he might be?"

Malina: "None at all, I'm afraid."

Servant: "I heard what happened at the tournament, seems so unfair."

Malina looked down sadly.

Malina: "He was so disappointed, so very angry. Oh how I wish I would have ran away with him."

Servant: "All will be well, my lady, you'll see. You will be the greatest queen Hispana will ever know."

Malina smiled.

Malina: "Thank you for the thought. I'm not really sure what I'd do if I were queen. All I know is that in my kingdom everyone will be happy, no one will be in need or want while I rule. I will unite the entire nation of Hispana, even the hostile provinces. At least I'll try."

Servant: "Highness? Could I try one of your dresses?"

Malina looked up at the servant.

Servant: "Oh, forgive me your majesty! I spoke out of place."

Malina smiled.

Malina: "It's alright. You know, I'm an only child. I've always wanted a sister.

(a knock at the door)

Malina: "Come in."

A lady servant enters.

"Your majesty?"

Malina: "Yes Nani?"

Nani: "Highness, dinner will be served shortly."

Malina: "Thank you Nani. Send word to my father, the king, that I'll be down soon."

Nani: "As you wish my lady."

Malina rose from her chair and looked at herself in the mirror. She walked to the door and turned around.

Malina: "Yes Simona, you may try on one of my dresses. Let's have a get-together soon. Maybe have a picnic or a walk by the lake, how's that sound?"

Simona stared at the princess.

Simona: "That would be lovely your highness, lovely."

Malina smiled at her and left downstairs. Simona turned and faced the long mirror.

Simona: "Yes, my dear sister. I can't wait."

Princess Malina slowly walked down the hallway leading up to the banquet hall. Her beauty was absolutely enchanting. Her long black hair hung from the side of her neck over her shoulder. She wore a bright white gown that, according to legend, once belonged to a princess of Baghdad that was given as a gift to the Hispana royal family decades ago by the sultan as an act of kindness and appreciation for the two nation's trading interests. A long ivory train draped over her shoulder. People were in awe, they were amazed at her presence. King Esteban walked toward his daughter and stretched out his hand. Princess Malina took her father's hand and slowly went down the few remaining steps of the stairway. Musicians played their harps and flutes. People murmured amongst themselves,

["Look, she is wearing the Gown of Legend."]

["She wears the attire of Princess Zayida-Yafiah!"]

King Esteban: "My, how you look. Your mother would be so proud."

Malina: "How I wish she was here."

King Esteban: "When all this is over, we will see her again. I promise."

Malina: "I know Father."

Everyone was happy. They all shouted,

["GOD BLESS THE KING! GOD BLESS PRINCESS MALINA OF HISPANA!"]

Everyone cheered.

"Your highness?"

Princess Malina turned around.

Malina: "Gali! You're here!"

The old Don happily embraced the princess.

King Esteban: "Welcome Gali, I'm delighted you came."

Gali: "How could I refuse the princess' invitation? I am honored."

King Esteban: "Please, let us sit. Let us dine."

Gali: "Sire."

Gali bowed his head in respect. Princess Malina smiled happily. It was a special moment for her.

Later on, after the feast, Malina walked out onto the open balcony of the castle. She gazed up at the beautiful full moon. The wind gently brushed against her face. She closed her eyes and thought of Alberto. How she loved him so. *Where could he be?* She wondered yearningly.

"Alberto?"

Alberto turned and saw his enchanting princess looking at him. Alberto smiled.

Alberto: "Malinali?"

Malina ran to embrace her handsome knight. Alberto hugged his princess tightly.

They looked deep into each other's eyes.

Alberto: "My love."

Alberto kissed Malina softly. As he slowly pulled away, Malina quickly leaned herself toward him and kissed Alberto again.

Alberto: "Malina, I..."

Malina: "Alberto, it's not your fault. You won the match. You won."

Alberto: "But I didn't win you."

Malina: "You've won me already, my love."

Alberto: "But not in court Malina! Not in the eyes of the realm! I may as well be a commoner like before!"

Malina looked at Alberto.

Alberto: "Nothing has gone as it should have. All this is just an unpalatable reality. I've failed you. I'm no knight at all."

Malina: "Stop it Alberto! Do not berate yourself, do you hear? You fought gallantly and I'm proud of you."

Malina gently placed her hands on Alberto's face and looked at him.

Malina: "I love you. I love you Alberto. Never forget that."

Alberto: "And I love you Malinali. You are my only one. You are the air that I breathe, the soul of my life."

Malina laid her head on Alberto's chest.

Malina: "Hold me, my love. Just hold me."

Alberto held her close. He gently caressed her long hair.

Alberto: "Run away with me?"

Malina looked up at him.

Malina: "Alberto, I..."

Alberto: "Forgive me, my love. I shouldn't have said that. It's not fair to you. Were you any other girl, I know you wouldn't hesitate. But you're not just any girl or lady, you're the princess of a kingdom, of a nation."

Alberto looked at Malina. His face only inches away from hers.

Alberto: "There's nowhere we could hide that you would not be found."

Malina: "My love, I'm sorry."

Alberto: "It's alright Malina. It's alright."

Malina: "What will you do?"

Alberto: "I don't know. I know I can't stay here any longer."

Malina: "My love."

Malina kissed Alberto deeply.

Alberto: "You keep stealing kisses."

Malina stared at her knight. His emerald eyes gazed back.

Alberto: "I must go."

Malina: "Don't go."

Alberto: "I must, if only a while."

Malina: "Alberto, no."

Alberto: "Please Malinali, try to understand. There is no place for me here."

Malina: "Don't leave me! I won't let you!"

Alberto took Malina's hand and kneeled on the floor. He softly kissed her hand as any knight would to his queen or princess.

Alberto: "It has been an honor serving you, your majesty."

Malina cried. Alberto arose and walked away.

Malina: "Alberto! No! Come back!"

Malina ran to Alberto. She wrapped her arms around him. Alberto looked at her.

The pain was too much to bear.

Alberto: "Malina, please. Let me go."

Malina: "Don't go."

Alberto: "Malina, let go of me."

Malina: "I won't let you go Alberto. I won't."

Alberto tried to release Malina's grip. She would not budge. She was determined to hold on to the love of her life.

Alberto: "Let go of me Malina, please my love."

Malina: "I won't let you go! I won't..."

Alberto: "Enough! Let go of me!"

Alberto freed himself. Malina slowly dropped to her knees, her eyes filled with tears. Alberto continued moving forward. Tears watered his eyes. They streamed down his cheeks endlessly. How he loved Malina! How he loved his princess! His heart broke in two, shattered. The parting between them was as a nail ripping from the flesh! Malina stared at the moon. It shone ever so brightly. Gali entered onto the balcony.

Gali: "Absolutely beautiful, isn't it?"

Malina: "Very, sometimes I wish there was more than one."

Gali: "Interesting concept highness. However, I think one is enough and far more than we deserve."

Malina smiled.

Gali: "I thank you for the invitation highness."

Malina: "Thank you for coming, Don Gali."

Gali: "But I know dinner wasn't the only reason you summoned me, your majesty."

Malina looked at Don Gali. Gali looked at the princess and then faced the moon once more. Malina sighed.

Malina: "You always know my mind Gali."

Gali: "How may I be of service?"

Malina: "I'm worried about the kingdom. I'm worried about the country as a whole."

Gali: "I understand."

Malina: "Will Hispana survive? Can you save us Gali?"

Gali "My powers are not what they once were highness. But I promise you I will do my utmost to defend our nation."

Malina: "I hear the pagan Emirs have their wizards and sorcerers as well."

Gali: "They do. In fact, Endora is on their side."

Malina looked at Gali, surprised.

Malina: "Endora? The Witch of Sevi?"

Gali: "Tis true, majesty."

Malina: "I should have known sooner or later they would have called upon her."

Gali walked to the opposite side of Malina.

Gali: "She is a mystery, this witch. Her origins are unknown. Some say she came from the land of the carpenter. Others say she first appeared in the ancient valley of the Basque regions."

Malina: "Or she came from the land of Sevi? Our southern region in Andalusia?"

Gali nodded in agreement.

Gali: "Perhaps, but no one is certain. Either way, she has never rested from trying to conquer Hispana. She is an evil one."

Malina: "And to think she once served my father."

Gali: "That was many stars ago. But she has come back and we must be cautious at all times from now on."

Malina: "And what of our allies?"

Gali: "I'm afraid our allies in Gaul cannot come to our aid. There is much political unrest in the senate council and their armies are already battling the barbarian hordes of Germania."

Malina: "I see."

Gali "I am keeping watch highness, do not worry."

Malina: "There is something else."

Gali: "Yes?"

Malina: "Father is not well. He has a coughing sickness. I noticed it when we went to market the other day. He assures me all is well, but I fear it is not. Is there anything you can give him?"

Gali: "Yes Highness. I shall have something for him upon my return. Be at peace."

Malina: "You have served my father well, Don Gali. The whole kingdom would be at a loss without you. Thank you."

Gali bowed before the princess.

Gali: "It is my life's honor, your majesty."

Malina: "I will retire for the night. Thank you again Gali."

Gali: "Before you retire highness, some friends would like to say hello."

Malina: "Who? Wait, don't tell me."

Gali: "Behind you."

Malina slowly turned around. She was overjoyed when two giant dragons steadily hovered above the open balcony.

Malina: "Antonio! Milagro!"

Antonio: ["Greetings your majesty! Good to see you again!"]

Malina: "Oh, Antonio! It's good to see you! I've missed you!"

Milagro puffed smoke at Antonio.

Milagro: ["Uh, (puff!) it's my turn to greet the princess!"]

Antonio grinned his giant sharp teeth at Milagro.

Malina: "Milagro! So good to see you too! I've missed you both!"

Milagro: ["Uh, it's… (puff!) it's good to… it's good to see you too, your majesty! (puff!)"]

Malina laughed happily. She loved her two Spano dragons. Gali smiled.

Gali: "Her highness is retiring for the night. Say goodnight. Perhaps you'll see her again tomorrow."

Milagro: ["G… goodnight y… your majesty!"]

Malina: "Aww Milagro. Goodnight sweetie."

Antonio: ["Goodnight highness! Sleep well!"]

Malina: "Goodnight my friends. I love you both."

Milagro: ["We (puff!) love you too highness!"]

Malina's heart sank. Seeing her two mystical dragons made her so happy.

Gali "Goodnight your majesty. Pleasant dreams."

Malina smiled and left.

Gali looked at the twin dragons.

Gali: "To the temple!"

In the Strait of Gibraltar, a sail ship flows on the water in the middle of the night. Upon the vessel, a man stands on the bow and speaks to a small crowd of passengers.

"Now you know the truth. And as it is written, the truth shall set you free. I've already told you his name. I've already told you of what he wants from us. Again I encourage you, accept his precious gift of eternal salvation. Believe, just believe and he will change your life. You need not pay any price my friends. Christ has already paid it all in full. The choice is yours. Thank you."

A few people cheered. The rest of them murmured.

Captain: "Fine speech Alberto!"

Alberto turned.

Alberto: "Thank you Captain. I hope it encouraged you?"

Captain: "It was motivating. Let's put it that way."

Alberto: "We all need a stepping stone to start off from. But don't leave the man knocking on your door wait for too long."

Captain: "Well noted teacher."

Alberto smiled. He then greeted a few of the people. Alberto entered the ministry. He traveled far and around spreading the gospel of the man called 'Christ'. He became a 'teacher of the carpenter'. His crusade was nearly over. He was bound for Hispana on his vessel named "The Malina". Alberto looked up at the full moon. He thought of his beloved princess.

Alberto: "My princess, how I long to see you once more. Forgive me, my love."

Up in the high mountain terrain of the Pyr region, Gali resides deep inside his temple domain. Two giant beasts tower above him.

Gali: "And what have you learned?"

Antonio: ["The Moranic armies are setting sail already my lord. The Zor of Moroc confers with the Witch of Sevi."]

Milagro: ["She sc... (puff!) scares me! She is a bad witch!"]

Gali smiles at Milagro.

Antonio: ["They should reach our shores by tomorrow night."]

Gali: "I see. We must be ready to protect the kingdom when they arrive."

Antonio: ["Yes my lord!"]

Gali: "The Zor? How did he seem to you?"

Antonio looked down at the Don.

Antonio: ["He seems very confident my lord. They have a large and massive army."]

Gali: "Yes, no doubt. I have heard of him. A man of dark nobility, he is."

Antonio: ["There is one other thing, my lord."]

Gali "Yes?"

Antonio: ["I didn't want to say anything but I did happen to see their brimant of dragons."]

Gali: "Brimant of dragons?"

Milagro: ["Hmm... No problem. (puff!) We can take 'em!"]

Gali "Well, I'm not surprised. I expected as much. Moroc has always sought our destruction. Now the time has come where they feel they can. It will be a terrible war."

Antonio: ["We can win. I know we can."]

Gali nodded.

Gali: "I think we can too."

Antonio: ["We have our Dyno allies in the great valley of Aran. They're ready."]

Gali: "Good. We will need them. Send word."

Antonio: ["It may take a few days. The Aran is not only far but very deep in that certain region. It's very vast."]

Gali: "It's worth the risk. Go. And be careful."

Antonio nodded in agreement. The two dragons fly off. Gali walked out of the rock cave and came down the steps of stone. He looked up at the eerie night sky.

Gali: "Make haste my friends."

Hours later.

Sailor: "Captain!"

Captain: "What is it?"

Sailor: "Look, a ship."

Captain: "I can't see the sail!"

The strange ship approached closer. The clouds covered the moon, making it difficult to see. Alberto awoke.

Alberto: "What is it Captain? What's wrong?"

Captain: "A ship of some kind, it's too dark to see."

Alberto: "Fishermen, I'm sure."

Captain: "Perhaps, you do realize we are in perilous waters?"

Alberto: "The enemy knows not to tread on our division of the strait."

Captain: "Tell that to them."

Alberto: "What?"

Alberto turns.

Suddenly, torches lit up. To their horrified eyes, an entire fleet of Emir ships enclosed on them.

Alberto: "Lord help us."

Captain: "Alert the men! Prepare for battle!"

Sailor: "Yes, captain!"

One of the sailors lit an arrow and shot it in the sky.

Captain: "Well teacher, can your carpenter deliver us from this evil?"

Alberto: "Do not mock his name, captain. If it is His will that we perish this night, then I will gladly open my arms to His judgement."

The captain extended a sword to Alberto.

Captain: "Before or after you slaughter them?"

Alberto stared at the sword.

Captain: "Our nation is at stake, teacher. We are the only ones standing between them and our country. Will you fight or turn the other cheek?"

On top of the bow of the enemy ship, Tarak, the commander of the Emirs, spoke out.

Tarak: "Armies of Moroc! Hear me! Destiny awaits! The future is above us like the clouds of the sky! The time has come! Praise be to the One! The all-knowing, the all-merciful!"

The armies cheered their leader.

Tarak: "A hundred years ago, our holy prophet began the true faith! But unlike our holy prophet, we will not wait for our opponents to convert! No, We will force them! Either they will accept or die!"

The entire army roared with chants and praises.

Tarak: "It is the will of the One! We are the true heirs of the prophet! We will show the world who we are! Tonight, we start with the enemy nation of Hispana! ...Forward!"

Local villagers saw the flaming arrow pierce the sky. They knew the enemy had finally come. They went about the town warning everyone. People were frightened. Their doom was sealed!

The southern region of Hispana was vulnerable. The nation was divided by different kingdoms and political views. But the northern kingdoms of Castile, Aragon, Leon, and Asturias were the most powerful under the rule of King Esteban. The other small provinces were ruled by powerful lords and earls, not kings. They were old in age and had no male heirs to take over in their passing, including King Esteban. Such a circumstance gave Malina the right to the throne as future queen, even surpassing her mother Queen Ometea (her Tenician name, her Spanian name - Omeya). But for now, she was only a princess. However, once queen, she would have the power and authority to unite the entire nation as one whole kingdom. This law did not set well with everyone. One such person was Roderic. He ruled only one province in the southern central region. A hostile area in rebellion to the king. He called himself "the last king of the Goths".

"Dear husband? Come to bed already."

Roderic turns to his wife Egilona. She laid in bed naked with a fur blanket covering her almost completely.

Roderic: "I cannot sleep now, dear wife. Something is not right about this night."

Egilona: "How so? This night is just the same as any other night, a bit chilly perhaps."

Roderic sneered. He stood tall wearing a red and silver silk robe. Standing close by the door entrance of his mausoleum-like home of stone, he stared at his beautiful 'queen'. His expression was hard to define.

Roderic: "I'm glad to see you're always in a jovial mood, Egilona. But I've no time for such behavior."

Egilona: "And I remind myself why I married you, my dear. Because you've no time for such behavior."

Roderic chuckled. He looked out in the vast plains. He noticed a flaming torch swaying with the unending wind. It drew closer.

Egilona: "Roderic? What is it?"

Roderic: "Stay here, my queen. It's alright."

Roderic quickly came down the stone stairway and opened the door. A man stood in front of him.

Roderic: "What is it Jurgus?"

Jurgus: "My Lord! We've just received word the Emir armies have landed on our shores. They have surrounded the entire southern region! And more are on the way along with their Saracen warriors!"

Roderic: "Has this been confirmed?"

Jurgus: "On my honor, my lord. There is no mistake."

Roderic was stunned at the news.

Roderic: "Damn King Esteban! He calls himself a king? He is not worthy of the title! He leaves the south of Hispana unprotected!"

Jurgus: "What shall we do? We are doomed."

Roderic: "What can we do but wait?"

Jurgus: "My Lord?"

Roderic thought for a moment. His servant Jurgus tried to catch his breath.

Roderic: "Go and gather what men you can. Wait for me at the river of Guad. With the army I have I will oppose this raiding force. We will ride out and meet them."

Jurgus: "As you command, my lord."

Roderic: "Go! We've no time to lose!"

Jurgus ran off into the cold night.

Roderic: "Well, my dear King Esteban, this time the glory will be mine!"

Inside the caves of the dark Atlas Mountains of Moroc, sounds of wails and torment are heard from afar. The Witch of Sevi slowly walks to the great river of blood.

Witch: "In the abyss, in the abyss! Show me the face of the true princess!"

The red river boiled with steam. The face of Princess Malina came into view.

Witch: "Oh. how happy she is. So young, so lovely, so pure."

The river showed the princess sleeping soundly. The witch's eyes twitched with anger. She knelt down and dipped her hand in the river and drank.

Witch: "Well your highness, enjoy yourself for now. Tomorrow, a new dawn will dwell over the land. Darkness will overshadow your kingdom. A new nation will be born."

Malina's image disappeared. The river ran red once again.

Witch: "You will never be queen... Oh no, my promised one, she is mine. Mine! Ha, ha, ha, ha!"

Blood dripped from her mouth as she walked into the darkness.

The wind blew endlessly all through the night. The moon shined down on San Juan castle. Within the king's bedroom, the curtains swayed back and forth due to an open window. Nearby, the fireplace burnt rapidly keeping the entire room warm despite the wind. King Esteban slept quietly. Suddenly, he was awakened by a creaking sound. There was a prolonged squeaking noise coining from the massive fireplace, whose floor extended further into the room with its firepit in the center. The king slowly rose and sat up. His eyes widened when he saw the back wall slowly turn! A figure appeared walking past the side of the flaming pit.

King Esteban: "Who's there?"

The king's heart leaped as he heard footsteps approaching. He rubbed his eyes and saw a woman standing in front of him.

King Esteban: "Sonia?"

Sonia: "Yes, your majesty. It is I, only I."

The king's eyes narrowed.

King Esteban: "What are you doing here?"

Sonia: "Isn't it obvious?"

King Esteban: "Sonia, it's very late."

Sonia looked at the king.

Sonia: "I saw you at the banquet the other night and again tonight."

King Esteban: "Sonia, please."

Sonia: "You didn't notice me, my dear. I noticed you."

King Esteban: "Sonia."

Sonia: "I looked at you, but you didn't look at me."

King Esteban: "Sonia, I can't do this anymore."

Sonia: "You never once looked at me!"

King Esteban: "Keep your voice down!"

The king stared at Sonia, shivering slightly. Sonia continued staring back.

Sonia: "Well, my dear? Have you anything to say?"

King Esteban: "You know why, matters of state have kept me extremely occupied."

Sonia: "Don't use the Great War as an excuse to ignore me. I will not have it, do you hear?"

King Esteban coughed abruptly and took a slow deep breath. He sighed in relief.

King Esteban: "You know I've been ill. I can't do anything properly."

Sonia: "You haven't touched me in weeks and it's not because of your illness either. You're bored of me, aren't you?"

King Esteban: "Don't be ridiculous."

Sonia: "Yes, you're tired of me."

King Esteban: "It's not that. It's just..."

Sonia: "It's just what?"

King Esteban: "Nothing, it doesn't matter."

Sonia: "I don't please you anymore? Is that it?"

The king turned away. Strongly affronted, Sonia raised her night gown and climbed onto the king's bed.

King Esteban: "Sonia, please. Not tonight."

Sonia lifted her gown off and exposed her breasts. She straddled the king.

Sonia: "Make love to me Esteban."

King Esteban: "Please, Sonia."

Sonia: "I said take me!"

King Esteban looked at her. Sonia breathed heavily. She panted as the bed shook back and forth. The king breathed uneasily. Faster and faster the bed shook. She moved rapidly onto his thighs taking the rhythm to a deeper and faster plane. Sonia looked down at the king, sneering at him with contempt. The king gasped.

Sonia: "And how is your lovely daughter?"

The king clenched his eyes tightly as he tried to repeatedly thrust into Sonia.

King Esteban: "Wha... wh... ugh!"

Faster and faster, Sonia shook the king until he finally released inside her. Sonia gasped and laughed at the same time. Sweat dripped from her forehead down to her cheeks.

Sonia: "Ah, my old man can still do it! Ha, ha, ha!"

King Esteban breathed sharply.

King Esteban: "Wha... what did you... what did you say about my daughter?"

Sonia looked at him.

Sonia: "You see my dear? You were able to come inside me."

The king's eyes closed slowly.

Sonia: "Fifteen years ago you came inside me. Remember my love?"

King Esteban: "What? I... uh."

Suddenly, the king coughed loudly. He gasped harshly. Sonia just stared at him.

King Esteban: "So... Sonia, my vial... please."

Sonia looked to the side of her. A small glass vial stood on the edge of the dresser. Sonia reached for it. The king continued to cough over and over again. The vial's top cap had a string tied to it. Sonia dangled it in midair.

Sonia: "Is this what you need, my dear?"

The king's coughing spasm grew worse.

King Esteban: "Sonia... my vial. P... please."

The king tried to get out of bed. Sonia shoved him back.

King Esteban: "Sonia! Wha... uh... [COUGH! COUGH!]"

Sonia: "It was I who should have been queen! Not your indigenous native bitch!"

King Esteban: "Ugh... Sonia..."

Sonia slapped King Esteban across the face. The king coughed out thick phlegm and soon blood.

Sonia: "Simona is our daughter! Do you hear me, your majesty?"

King Esteban: "It... can't be..."

Sonia: "She is! And I'm going to restore her birthright!"

The king's face turned pale.

King Esteban: "M... Malina..."

Sonia: "No, Malina is no more, highness. She will not rule for long."

King Esteban: "Ugh... n... no... ugh..."

King Esteban drew his last breath. He died with his eyes open. Sonia looked at him and grinned. She reached to the back of her hair and pulled out a sharp pin. She stared at it.

Sonia: "Well? Guess I didn't need you after all then."

She stepped down from the king's bed. She took her gown and walked back to the secret entrance of the fireplace naked. She disappeared from sight as the stone wall slowly turned back in place.

Flames consumed a burning ship. The high mast came falling down along with a torn sail. Alberto's vessel, "The Malina" was no more. He looked sadly as it perished beneath the waters.

Tarak: "'The Malina'? Nice name. After the princess of Aragon, no doubt?"

Tarak stared at Alberto. He noticed his necklace bearing the shape of a fish, a Christian symbol.

Tarak: "Nothing to say 'teacher'? Ha, ha, ha!"

Alberto looked down silently. The Emirs killed almost everyone on board the ship. They plundered goods and took captives, Alberto among them. Most of the Emirs wore black with turbans around their heads, some with their faces nearly covered.

Tarak: "Where is your god?"

Alberto: "In my heart. Where is yours?"

An Emir soldier strikes Alberto. Blood streams down his bruised face.

Tarak: "Well? In answer to your question, who's the victor here? Hmm?"

Alberto looked at the Emir leader.

Alberto: "My God is able to deliver me, I do not fear you."

Tarak: "You Christians really amuse me. To worship a carpenter? I ask you again. Where is your god? Is he away making a table perhaps? Or building a house for someone?"

All the pagan Emirs laughed loudly.

Alberto: "Mock him all you want, pagan. Someday he will return. He promised."

Tarak laughed.

Tarak: "Is that all your god is? A carpenter?"

Alberto: "No, he is much more. He is the promised one, the savior of all men."

Tarak: "I'll haggle with you no further. It's obvious whose god is real and whose isn't."

Alberto looked at Tarak boldly. The Emir leader drew his sword and placed it upon Alberto's throat. The two stared into each other's eyes with a baleful glare. Finally, Tarak lowered his sword and sheathed it.

Tarak: "I admire your bravery, teacher. I've seen Christians before. You are no ordinary Christian."

There was a loud screech high in the sky. Everyone looked at the heavens. A whole brimant of dragons cut through the night sky with Emir sorcerers and wizards mounted on them. Tarak smirked insolently.

Tarak: "The rest of our army. Soon, they should reach the northern part of Hispana and destroy all the kingdoms within."

Alberto closed his eyes and sighed.

Tarak: "Come teacher, we've a new crusade to embark."

The Emir army continued its quest toward the nation of Hispana.

"THE KING IS DEAD! LONG LIVE THE QUEEN!"

The entire royal assembly repeated the chant twice more. A grief-stricken Malina tried to compose herself calmly. It was two days later after the death of King Esteban when he was found by maidservants.

Xitl: "Highness? Are you alright? You don't have to do this."

Malina sighed softly.

Malina: "I'm fine Xitl. Thank you. I have to do this."

Xitl bowed his head.

Malina opened the curtains and walked through with ease. She looked out and stared at everyone, every royal official was present. Malina stepped onto the podium chamber.

Malina: "Hispanians! I thank you all for being here! As you know, my father, your king, passed away two days ago. His majesty died from an unknown coughing sickness. It is a sad day for all of us here, a sad day for all Hispana. Especially now since the Great War is upon us! A poor time indeed."

All eyes of the assembly carefully studied Malina.

Malina: "All of our northern armies have already assembled their forces. The Emir army has invaded our shores with a conquering force. A sworn enemy and lasting foe from the land of Moroc! We always knew this day would come. We will defend our kingdom and our country. I ask Senor Martin de la Garza to come forward!"

All was calm. Out of the crowd stepped forth an elegantly dressed gentleman in uniform. He bent down on one knee, bowed his head, and looked up at Malina.

Malina: "Senor Martin, you have always served my father well. I now ask of your service to devote yourself, your skills, and your life on behalf of the nation of Hispana, in her defense. What say you, sir knight?"

Senor Martin: "It would be my honor, your majesty! My life's honor!"

Malina: "Senor Martin! I now declare you High Commander General of the entire northern army of Hispana!"

Senor Martin once again bowed his head in respect to the princess who was now queen.

Malina: "Arise, sir knight and be recognized!"

All the royal assembly applauded as the new commander stood up. Martin raised his arm and waved at the royal assembly.

Later in Malina's royal chamber room, Malina sat upon her high throne discussing matters with her royal council. Gali the Don of Villalobos and her loyal Aztec friend Xitl were also present.

Malina: "It pains me to say, I have no choice but to postpone the coronation of the crown until all this calms down."

Gallegos: "Majesty, I think that would not be wise."

Malina: "Why do you think so Gallegos?"

Gallegos: "Your majesty, with respect, the king is no more. Your mother, the queen is away in her homeland. You are now queen of Hispana. Hence, we cannot afford to wait on this important matter."

Oliveros: "If her majesty wishes to wait on her crown, then let it be so. I see no reason for haste."

Gallegos looks at Oliveros.

Gallegos: "Have you forgotten we are at war? And if by the devil's chance Hispana should fall, what then? A nation perishes without an official queen of the realm? I say no!"

Oliveros: "If by the devil's chance the kingdom should fall and the nation perishes, what difference would it make then whether the realm has an official queen or not?"

Gallegos: "It's a matter of honor, a matter of prestige. Highness, I urge you not to wait. You must seize the crown."

Oliveros: "And my council is to wait. Her highness is dealing with other pressing matters at the moment. She just lost her father and she is responsible for protecting an entire nation, let alone a kingdom."

Gallegos: "At most, it would be merely a formality, a matter of propriety. Not to mention traditional and may I add, sentimental and affectionate value to the realm. The coronation must be official."

Oliveros: "Her majesty doesn't need an official coronation to be recognized as queen. She is queen!"

Gallegos: "I protest! I..."

Malina: "Gentlemen, gentlemen, please. I thank you both for your council. You've both made good points on this subject. Let me think some more on this matter, I beg you. The funeral ceremony is tomorrow. I'll deal with this later."

Gali: "Her highness is tired, my lords. I think she requires some rest, don't you?"

Gallegos and Count Oliveros nodded in agreement.

Gallego: "Majesty, again, I'm sorry for your loss. With your highness' permission, I will take my leave."

Malina: "You may. Thank you Gallegos."

Gallegos bowed and departed. Count Oliveros stood before Malina and kneeled.

Oliveros: "The queen of Hispana needs beg to no one, highness."

Malina: "I thank you deeply Count Oliveros. You may go."

The count bowed his head and left.

Malina sighed. She was overwhelmed.

Gali: "Are you well, Highness?"

Malina: "Yes, Don Gali. Thank you."

Gali bowed.

Xitl: "Highness? A messenger."

Malina nodded and waved the messenger to enter. The messenger approached before Malina and knelt to the floor.

Malina: "Arise. What news?"

The messenger opened the parchment scroll.

Messenger: "The war report, your majesty."

Malina: "Go on."

Messenger: "The Emirs have sacked the southern part of Hispana."

Malina: "Andalusia?"

Messenger: "Yes highness. According to our scouts, they have set up a prison base in Cordoba. Also our forest men are fighting the Emir sorcerers and dragons."

Malina: "And what of our goods?"

Messenger: "Trade has halted due to the war, majesty. Many of our ships carrying our supplies haves ceased. Even independent vessels have been plundered and destroyed. Here is a list of some ships: 'La Dona,' 'El Gigante,' 'La Madre,' and..."

The messenger stopped. Malina looked at him.

Malina: "And?"

Messenger: "And 'La Malina,' your majesty."

Malina was stunned. A ship named after her? Only one name entered her mind. Alberto. No. it couldn't be. Was it possible?

Malina: "And what of the members on board?"

Messenger: "It's uncertain who survived and who did not majesty. But if any are alive, most likely they'll be imprisoned in Cordoba."

Malina: "Where in Cordoba?"

Messenger: "Our scouts say in the valley of Paz, highness."

Malina: "Do you know what kind of ship 'La Malina' was?"

The messenger looked down into the scroll.

Messenger: "An independent sail ship purchased for traveling to the Holy Land, highness. Apparently used for evangelism."

Gali: "I've heard of these vessels, your majesty. The men who sail these are called 'teachers of the faith'."

Malina looked down.

Malina: "Is there anything more?"

Messenger: "That is all highness."

Malina: "You may go."

The messenger bowed and left the royal chamber. Malina arose from her throne and softly stepped down and paced the floor nervously.

Gali: "Xitl, could you give us a moment alone?"

Xitl: "Of course, Don Gali."

Xitl left the room. Gali looked at Malina.

Malina: "You always know my mind Gali."

Gali "Yes highness, I do and this time I must disagree."

Malina: "What if he's alive? Imprisoned?"

Gali: "Highness?"

Malina turned and looked at Gali.

Malina: "I have to know Gali."

The old wizard looked at Malina. He could see she was determined to find her love Alberto.

Gali: "No, highness. You're too important to risk. If something were to happen to you, what then? You are the only heir!"

"I beg to differ!"

Gali and Malina turn in surprise. Sonia and Simona approach them.

Gali: "What is the meaning of this?"

Sonia: "A family affair, wizard! Nothing to do with you."

Xitl: "Sorry highness! They went right past me."

Malina: "It's alright, Xitl. Wait outside."

Xitl: "Yes majesty."

Malina looks at the two women with curiosity.

Malina: "Please explain yourself, Sonia."

Sonia: "With pleasure, your majesty. And I might add, that was what your father, the king, gave me for fifteen years."

Malina: "What? How dare you!"

Sonia: "Oh, it's true highness. I was his whore ever since I came to San Juan castle."

Malina: "My father?"

Sonia: "Yes highness, your father. He coveted me and took me as his own whenever he wished. Thus impregnating me with our lovely daughter Simona.... your half-sister."

Malina looked at Simona. Simona smirked.

Simona: "Greetings my older sister."

Malina looked at her boldly with disbelief.

Simona: "Looks like I'll be taking those walks by the lake by myself."

Gali looked at Sonia.

Gali: "Do you have any proof of these accusations?"

Sonia: "As a matter of fact I do. Years ago, I kept a diary detailing all my comings and goings with the king. You can see them if you like? The dates and writings are accurate in years and were not forged this morning. The journal itself has aged."

Sonia shows Gali the diary book. Malina is stunned. She instantly recognizes the engraved cover.

Malina: "That was my mother's! How did you get it?"

Sonia: "It wasn't difficult."

Malina: "Get out! I want you out of my castle!"

Sonia: "Very well. But know this, I will make this a public matter. The whole kingdom will know the truth about your father. Do not think I am unprepared highness."

Malina: "Get out!"

Simona: "I will have my birthright, dear sister. I will come back and take what's rightfully mine!"

Simona and Sonia leave.

Malina: "Gali?"

Gali: "I had no knowledge of this highness."

Malina sighed. She could not believe this dreaded news and the scandal it would cause. Not now, not in the middle of a national war!

Alberto lay fast asleep in a high tower of a cathedral, just one of the many structures the pagan Emirs captured and used as one of their prison bases. Why build prison camps or towers from the ground up when you can conquer and take what's already there and use it for your desire? Alberto awoke to the sound of chirping and cooing. Could it be birds singing? He rose up from his cot and walked close to the edge of the open window, too small and narrow for him to slip through for an escape. Yes, the thought had entered his mind numerous times. A little bit wider than a slit, the window was. Oddly enough, the church was once a prison, now a cathedral. Ironic that it was now back in use as its original intention. Alberto noticed two birds eating the crumbs of bread on the edge of the window. This surprised Alberto. How did the crumbs of bread get onto the edge? He did not put them there. The birds had to have come down onto the floor to pick them up with their beaks and go back up onto the edge. He noticed the birds were pigeons! As he stepped closer, the birds instantly became afraid and flew off.

The next day, an Emir guard brought Alberto some food. Alberto took his tray from under the opening of the tower door. He quickly ate his meal. Afterward, he broke pieces of bread and placed them carefully, leading from the window down across the floor by his cot. Alberto hoped the pigeons would return soon.

The days passed. The war raged on as the Emir armies conquered the entire south of Hispana. They were slowly making their way up toward the north. The great and sudden responsibility of being queen drained Malina emotionally, but she was strong-willed and focused on taking care of her kingdom. But the overwhelming invading armies was just one of Malina's problems at court. Sonia, the former servant of the king brewed more trouble by making public her affair with King Esteban. She made it seem as if she was the victim, as if she was an unwilling partner forced to lay with the king or face hunger and fiending for herself in the streets of villages or die starving in the forests and valleys.

Sonia: "My fellow countrymen! I have here a written document by the king's own hand, acknowledging our illicit affair and giving notice of titleship to our daughter Simona, who is an innocent victim of this scandal! The king recognizes his illegitimate daughter and grants her the title as princess of Hispana! I appeal to you, the people, to help us make this right! Allow my daughter, King Esteban's second born, to be instated as a princess of Castile or Leon or Galicia, since Malina already has Aragon. She is the king's daughter! She has a God given right to her title of 'princess'! Help us!"

Sonia was indeed prepared for the public scandal just as she told Malina. After fifteen years of being the king's mistress, she was very well-endowed. During the years of the secret affair, the king would give Sonia jewelry, rings, diamonds, rubies, and gold coins. It was more than enough to live comfortably for many years.

Malina: "The people are restless, riots are forming, laws are being broken. I even had to send out some of my personal guards to police the surrounding areas and restore order. Oh Gali, what am I going to do? I admit, I'm too young to be queen. Sonia has created quite a stir with her claims about my father. The people are supporting her."

Gali: "Majesty, you are doing fine, just fine. We are all here for you, to help guide you."

Malina: "Any word on Antonio and Milagro?"

Gali: "I've sent them on a mission to secure certain allies."

Malina: "I'm afraid for them."

Gali: "They'll be fine, highness. Do not worry."

Malina: "Sonia has said she has proof in writing that my father admits to this scandal."

Gali: "Yes, Count Oliveros has already seen the document and swears it is not the king's handwriting. He contests it."

Malina looks at the bearded wizard.

Malina: "A forgery?"

Gali "However, it matters not because it bears the king's ring seal."

Malina: "The king's seal? But how? No one can approach the king or take anything from his person without his permission or knowing about it."

Gali looked at his queen.

Gali "Then how did she get the symbol of the seal on paper? Either the king himself stamped his ring on the parchment or she took it from him personally and did it herself."

Malina: "And the only way to do that is... is to be near him. Next to him, with him knowing full well and with open mind."

Gali stared at Malina. It seemed that even if the document was false, the affair was the truth. Malina realized if what Sonia said was true, then Simona was indeed her half-sister and therefore rightfully a princess by birth. Malina was no fool. As she stated to her father once, she knew somewhat the ways of the world. Looking back, she now recalled some odd moments in her father's behavior toward her mother Queen Omeya and how he shunned her at times. She remembered all too well how he would laugh with glee whenever Sonia was serving him at court. Only now were Malina's eyes really opening. It was disappointing, but she loved her father and nothing, no matter what he did, changed that.

Early the next morning, as Malina ate breakfast in bed, a small pigeon appeared on the ledge of her window. Malina sighed in surprise.

Malina: "Hello, how are you?"

The bird cooed.

Malina: "Where did you come from?"

Malina noticed a piece of thread tied around the pigeon's neck. It looked as though it came from a piece of clothing. To her surprise, a piece of ivory cloth was rolled up inside the tied thread. Malina gently took hold of the pigeon's neck and undid the thread tied knot. She slowly opened the cloth. Her eyes widened.

The cloth had a message, a message in blood! It read:

"Malina, I'M ALIVE AT CATHEDRAL TOWER IN CORDOBA, PAZ VALLEY.

ALL MY LOVE, Alberto."

Malina recognized the piece of torn cloth. She saw the embroidery on the edge. It was from the long scarf she gave Alberto moments before the joust tournament. Malina's heart melted. She closed her eyes and sighed happily.

Malina: "Alberto, my love, my life."

Malina presented Gali with the torn, bloody message.

Gali: "In his own blood?"

Malina: "Yes."

Gali stared at the message.

Gali: "This confirms the report of the pagan Emirs setting their prison base in the Paz Valley of Cordoba."

Malina: "I wonder how the bird was able to find me?"

Gali: "That is the mystery of these so called 'carrier pigeons'. Some say they can find their destination or person simply by scent. Prior to staining this cloth with his blood, Alberto must have waved your perfume cloth on the bridge of the bird's nose."

Malina looked at Gali.

Malina: "There is no mistake. I must save him Gali."

Gali looked at Malina.

Malina: "Help me."

Gali sighed.

Gali "Very well, where is the pigeon?"

Malina: "Here."

Gali: "We must respond. Dip your feather into the ink and write a small message on the back of the same cloth."

Malina: "The same?"

Gali "Yes, his blood is the scent the bird already recognizes."

Malina quickly dipped her writing feather in the black ink bottle and wrote her message. Gali read the message, rolled it up, and securely tied the torn cloth onto the pigeon's neck with a clean thin ribbon. Gali motioned Malina to gently grab hold of the winged messenger. Malina took the bird in her hands and calmly walked to the open window.

Malina: "Godspeed little one!"

Malina raised her hands and set the carrier pigeon loose. The bird took flight. Later that night, Gali returned to San Juan castle. He pulled forth a scrolled map and showed Malina. She looked earnestly.

Gali: "Majesty, here is a regional map of our area. This is our location."

Malina curiously studied the parchment drawn map.

Gali: "We are here. According to this map, it shows Alberto is somewhere here. There is a way to the Paz valley without being seen from enemy forces."

Malina: "Which way?"

Gali points toward the map.

Gali: "Here, through the forbidden land of Sogo."

Malina: "Sogo?"

Gali: "Yes highness."

Malina: "That's the province my father demilitarized. Set up a de facto wall around the city."

Gali: "A rebellious people, the Sogs. Not so much against the crown, but against our Lord and his laws."

Malina: "Yes, they rally quite often. Always demanding certain rights of equality. But to no avail."

Gali nodded his head in agreement.

Malina: "Their morals will never enter my kingdom."

Gali: "As your father wished it so, your majesty."

Malina: "Tell me more."

Gali: "There are tunnels deep in the plateau hills. Due to massive earthquakes, caverns were formed underneath. Thus, creating numerous passageways."

Malina: "Thank God for that."

Gali: "So far almost no one knows of these pathways, highness."

Malina: "Who else?"

Gali: "As far as I know? Myself, your majesty, and Endora."

Malina looked at Gali.

Malina: "The Witch of Sevi?"

Gali nodded.

Malina: "And by now the Zor of Moroc, no doubt!"

Gali: "Perhaps."

Malina: "Heaven forbid, the entire Emir army also?"

Gali: "Majesty, it can still be used to our advantage. But only if we hurry."

Malina: "When do we leave?"

Gali: "Tonight."

And so the journey began. Malina declared Count Oliveros temporary regent of Hispana until her return. The count accepted with honor. Gali brought his long carriage with a team of horses and two apprentices to help him along the way.

Malina was ready. Her entourage consisted of Gali the Wizard, also known as the Don of Villalobos, his two apprentices Enrique and Damian, Xitl the Aztec eagle warrior, and a jaguar knight named Tlaxca who previously sailed from the nation of Tenoc to serve Malina's family as an elite guardsman. An entire day had passed. Malina awoke from her nap. She saw the old wise wizard sitting across from her.

Gali: "Good morning highness."

Malina: "Good morning Gali."

Gali: "Did her majesty sleep well?"

Malina: "I prefer my bed in the palace."

Gali laughed.

Malina: "I wish Antonio and Milagro were here with us. The trip would be much quicker."

Gali: "So do I."

Malina: "I know they're out there fighting in this war against the brimants of Emir dragons. Oh, their dragon hordes are deadly and fierce but so are Antonio and Milagro. I shouldn't underestimate them."

Gali: "Antonio and Milagro can hold their own, majesty. Have no fear."

Malina: "Such a lovely day."

Gali: "We'll stop and rest in the next village."

Malina: "Thank you for everything Gali."

Gali smiled.

Gali: "Nothing highness, nothing at all."

Malina yawned and went back to sleep. They traveled far from the kingdom and deep into the heart of central Hispana. Their destination grew close. The long, four-door carriage came to a stop. Enrique and Damian stepped down from the driver's seat. Xitl and Tlaxca looked out the window. Gali opened the door and looked around.

Gali: "The demilitarized de facto wall up ahead."

Malina looked out.

Malina: "SogoSogo?"

Gali: "Sogo. From here we go on foot."

The night approached quickly. Malina grew tired but her eagerness to save Alberto gave her strength. She could suddenly feel his presence somehow, that gave her hope. They slowly drew nearer to the wall of Sogo.

"ALTO! WHO GOES THERE?"

Two guardsmen approached the six pilgrims, swords in hand. Xitl and Tlaxca raised their maqua-huitl weapons, ready to defend Malina.

"I SAID, WHO GOES THERE?"

Gali: "A servant of the most high! Lower your weapons!"

The guards laughed.

"NO ONE COMES HERE WITHOUT AUTHORIZATION OLD MAN!"

Gali waved his hands in the air. Suddenly, the two guardsmen became paralyzed! Their feet stuck and rooted into the ground, their swords fall to the ground.

"WHO ARE YOU? HOW DARE YOU COME HERE! WE ARE DEFENDING THE QUEEN'S REALM! RELEASE US WIZARD!"

Gali: "Then be at peace, gentlemen. I too am here on her majesty's service. What is your name?"

"I am the arch-guardsman Michael."

"And I am the arch-guardsman Gabriel. We serve the queen of Hispana and only the queen."

Gali: "Then we are on the same team."

Gali turned. Malina approached the two arch-guardsmen. She slowly pulled back her drape-hooded cape. The two guards saw the beauty of the young lady in front of them wearing a thin sparkling crown on her head.

Michael: "Your majesty!"

Gabriel: "Highness!"

Malina: "My thanks gentlemen."

Michael: "I… uh... I would be happy to kneel highness. But as you can see, we are stuck."

Malina smiled. She turned and looked at Gali.

Gali: "Upon your order, majesty?"

Malina nodded her head. That's all it took. The wizard released his spell and the two guards fell to their knees in fealty.

Malina: "Arise."

Michael and Gabriel rise.

Michael: "May I ask, majesty, where do you venture?"

Malina was about to speak, but then remembered Gali saying hardly anyone knew of the deep tunnels. She wasn't sure if it was wise to reveal their location. Malina looked toward Gali.

Gali: "We seek passage to the underground caverns. I regret to reveal their existence."

Gabriel: "Underground caverns?"

Gali: "Yes."

Michael: "I've heard of such caverns. But no one knows where they are my lord."

Gali: "Good thing I do and I hope it stays that way."

Michael and Gabriel look at each other.

Michael: "We swear to say nothing my lord."

Gabriel: "We will guide you through, my lord. But once you pass the gate, we cannot protect you."

Gali looked at Gabriel.

Gabriel: "Not that you need much protection."

Gali: "You're just performing your duties. I can respect that and so does her highness."

Michael: "It's an honor to serve you, your majesty."

Malina: "You have my deepest gratitude and affection gentlemen. Thank you both."

The two guardsmen bowed in respect. Suddenly, a crowd of people gathered upon the wired gates yelling and screaming.

Michael: "Quickly! This way!"

An array of Sogs pounded and shook the wired part of the walled gate. Malina covered her head and quickly followed Gali. Xitl and the rest of her entourage followed in haste. A burst of activity grew out of control. The ferocious Sogs cried out blasphemies at them.

"WHO ARE THESE INTRUDERS?"

"WE WANT THEM!"

A female Sog noticed the lovely Malina before she covered her face.

"I LIKE HER! SHE'S PRETTY! I WANT HER! I WANT HER!"

The female Sog opened her vest, exposing her breasts. She shook them back and forth tauntingly. The Sogs were a rabid bunch. Malina could not believe that such behavior existed in a people. Men kissing men, women licking women, both

opposites abandoning the other for the same sex. Also incestuous brothers and sisters sleeping with each other and others who slept with their own animals. Day after day, the Sogs performed their indecent acts. Men manscaping other men with their teeth. Also engaging in sexual orgies in the blood pits and mud! It was a hideous sight! All in full view of the guards. They tolerated it. Their duty was to watch them to make sure they didn't cross over the security wall. The Sogs continued in their endless rants.

"SEND THEM IN!"

"SEND THEM IN, THAT WE MAY KNOW THEM!"

Suddenly, to Malina's horror, the wired gate broke and the rebellious people tried to break through in a desperate frenzy! Michael cried out to his men to control the situation. Several arch-guardsmen under Michael and Gabriel approached the fiery crowd with bats and shields, hitting them and sending them back into their imprisoned state. However, the rabble continued. Gali opened his long brown cloak and pulled forth a sack hanging from his belt and opened it.

Gali: "Give me your hands gentlemen, if you please."

Michael and Gabriel obeyed. They opened their hands. Gali carefully poured an element into each hand.

Michael: "What is this my lord?"

Gali: "Clear dust. Go to the gates and simply blow it out of your hand."

Michael: "But...?"

Gali: "It's alright, do as I say."

Michael and Gabriel bowed their heads. The two guards walked up to the gates.

Malina: "Gali?"

Gali "A moment, highness."

Malina stared at the gates where the uproar was taking place. Michael and Gabriel raised their open palms and blew the dust into the noisy crowd. A magical occurrence formed, the clear dust made its way into the eyes of the entire mob and blinded them! The people cried in horror. They could no longer see. The Sogs finally dispersed and gave up. All became quiet and peaceful once more. Michael and Gabriel could not believe it. They looked at the old wizard and waved gratefully.

Gali: "Come, we've still a long journey."

Malina and her friends followed the wise and powerful wizard into the night.

The next day, the Emir commander Tarak discusses withdrawal from the Paz Valley to fight in the Great War.

Soldier: "Let's burn the cathedral my lord, with every man inside."

Tarak laughs.

Tarak: "Gentlemen, gentlemen! You've no imagination! An excellent idea, but no. Far too common, far too easy, and far too simple. There is no challenge in that. No, I have a better idea."

The Emir army stands at attention outside the prison cathedral. Alberto glances through the narrow tower window and sees the entire army below. Tarak looks up at the tower.

Tarak: "Hispanians! The time has come for us to leave here! We go to fight in the Great War! Hear me! There will be no guards to attend to you! No one to feed you! You are all condemned to die! We leave you to starve!"

The prisoners shouted in fear. They cried out in disbelief.

"WHAT ABOUT WATER?"

"WE'LL DIE OF THIRST!"

Tarak: "Ask the Nazarene called Jesus to provide you with living water! Isn't that what he proclaims to be?"

The army laughed loudly.

Tarak: "Your country is no more! Hispana will perish! And it all starts with you!"

Tarak mounts his horse.

Tarak: "I bid thee farewell!"

Tarak waves his army to follow him. The Emirs abandon the Paz Valley. Alberto was sorrowful. He laid down on his cot to rest. He was too tired to worry about starvation at the moment. All he could think about is if Malina had received his message. He had hoped against all hope that she did. He closed his eyes and went to sleep. He dreamed of his beautiful princess.

{Psst! Malinali? Ma..."}

Alberto looked up at the lighted window. A lovely young maiden appeared smiling down at him. She threw down a long, golden-colored rope that was secured to an iron bar from inside the window. Alberto grabbed onto the rope and climbed up

the wall of the castle tower. Once inside, Alberto saw his beloved princess in front of him.

Alberto: "Malina?"

Malina smiled and ran to embrace her handsome knight.

Malina: "Alberto, my love."

Alberto: "I've missed you."

Malina: "And I you, sorry I couldn't get away sooner."

Alberto: "It's alright. We've both been busy. You being a princess, me being a knight."

Malina smiled. Alberto looked into her eyes.

Alberto: "Malina?"

Malina: "Yes?"

Alberto: "I've been wanting to ask you."

Malina: "Yes?"

Alberto looked down in hesitation. He then got down on one knee and looked up at his beloved princess.

Alberto: "Malina de Zaragoza, would you marry me?"

Malina gasped in surprise.

Malina: "Oh Alberto."

Malina turned in sorrow.

Alberto: "I'm sorry. I know I don't have a ring, but I..."

Malina: "It's not that. Yes, I'll marry you."

Alberto heard her, but did not believe her.

Alberto: "Yes? You'll marry me? But...?"

Malina: "A knight named Garcia has already asked my father for my hand in marriage."

Alberto: "Garcia? Adolfo Garcia?"

Malina: "Yes."

Alberto: "And what did the king say?"

Malina looked at Alberto.

Malina: "You know the laws of the kingdom. My father nor I have no say in the matter. If another knight disputes a knight's claim to a princess' hand, then the only way to settle the matter is by combat. Whoever wins, by law the princess of the realm shall be betrothed to him only."

Alberto looked down sadly.

Alberto: "Then I will challenge him to a duel."

Malina hugged Alberto tightly.

Malina: "My love, please. Let it not be by the sword."

Alberto: "Garcia is great with a sword and I respect him. Have no fear my love. I will choose by way of the joust."

Malina: "I'm sorry it has to be this way. I'm sorry for all this protocol and laws and..."

Alberto: "Shh! Malina, it's alright. I know no matter what happens, you will always be in my heart. I love you Malinali, forever."

Malina stared into Alberto's eyes. She raised her hands and untied her hair, pulling forth a long ivory silk cloth.

Malina: "I love you Alberto, forever. This is my favorite color. A knight can only go into combat wearing a lady's color. I will give this to you on the day of the joust."

Alberto: "So be it my lady, as you say."

Malina the princess and Alberto the knight kissed each other in an endless passion.

Later in the evening, Alberto awoke to a cooing sound. His heart leapt for joy! Could it be? It had to. He felt it deep inside. On the edge of the tower window was a bird. A pigeon! Was it the same one that carried his blood-stained message? He raised from his cot and slowly crept toward the cooing bird. He took hold of it and noticed the same cloth. He gently pulled forth the rolled message and opened it. Alberto smiled happily. Malina had indeed received his message!

The message read:

"My dearest Alberto,

I'm on my way to you. Gali the Wizard is with me. Be strong.

All my love,
Malina"

Alberto: "Praise be to you, Lord Jesus Christ! I thank you for these precious creatures!"

Alberto fell on his knees and thanked the Lord.

Deep in the caverns, everyone set up camp. Enrique lit up a fire. Damian double-checked the water bags. There was still enough for everyone. Malina laid down as comfortably as she could. At least she had her small pillow and a few blankets she had brought from the palace. She prayed before going to sleep.

Malina: "Heavenly Father, smile upon us and show us favor. In your holy name I pray, Amen."

Xitl took the first watch. Tlaxca slept with one eye open! It would be his turn in a few hours.

Gali: "You alright Xitl?"

Xitl: "Yes Don Gali. It's a bit dark, but the fire's close by. I'll be fine."

Gali took off his large balled ring.

Gali: "Here, place this on your finger."

Xitl: "My lord?"

Gali: "Raise it above you."

Xitl obeyed. He raised his hand. To his astonishment, the ring glowed bright shining a massive light!

Xitl: "Thank you Don Gali."

Gali smiled.

Gali: "It knows when to go off. Be sure to give it to Tlaxca on the next watch."

Xitl: "Yes Don Gali, thank you."

Gali: "Good night."

Xitl: "Good night."

All through the night, groans and cries were heard throughout the cathedral prison. Alberto was sad hearing the men crying for food and water, yearning for nourishment. It was a scary and uncomfortable feeling. But Alberto was full of hope. He knew Malina would come. He knew his princess would save him. She had to! He could feel her presence. Alberto looked out the thin and narrow tower window. He saw the beautiful full moon shining so ever bright.

Alberto: "Malina, my love, my life."

After a few days of traveling through the deep caverns of Sogo and inhospitable harsh lands of the Paz Valley, Malina had finally reached her destination!

Gali "There it is! The cathedral prison of Cordoba!"

Malina sighed in relief. Everyone looked in amazement.

Gali: "Listen to me, all of you. We must approach with caution. Your majesty, stay behind me."

Malina nodded.

Gali: "Enrique, Damian, to either side of me."

Enrique: "Yes, my lord."

Damian: "Yes, my lord Gali."

Gali: "Xitl, Tlaxca, behind the queen. Guard us from the rear."

Xitl and Tlaxca nodded in agreement. Gali slowly moved his hand in a circular motion. To the awe of everyone, a glass shield appeared. Gali motioned his hand four more times, thus creating four more glass-like shields. He gave the four shields to everyone guarding the princess, who was now queen.

Gali "Let us commence slowly."

They started walking toward the cathedral across the grassy plain. They would soon reach the dirt road leading all the way to the church prison.

Xitl: "Where is the army? Did they leave?"

Gali: "It would seem so. Strange that they would do that."

Malina: "I don't like it."

Gali: "It'll be alright."

The old village surrounding the cathedral was almost empty. The pagan Emirs destroyed everything in sight. Few people went about their usual business attending to chores and their work. They noticed the six pilgrims approaching the high and mighty cathedral doors. Gali looked up at the tall doors.

Gali: "Iron? No problem."

With a push of his hand in the air, the mighty cathedral doors opened wide! Gali led everyone through. He turned to Malina.

Gali: "Go find your Alberto, highness."

Malina smiled happily. She went toward the stone staircase which would lead up to the tower.

Gali: "Xitl, Tlaxca, go with her."

The two Aztec knights obeyed and followed their queen in haste. Gali looked around the cathedral and kept watch.

Malina: "Alberto! Alberto!"

Malina called Alberto's name over and over. The cries of his name awoke Alberto up from his sleep. He tried to get up. A few days of no food or water, he had begun to grow weak. Shouts from other prisoners also rang throughout the cathedral tower, begging to be freed.

Malina: "Alberto! WHERE ARE YOU?"

Alberto tried to shout, but his mouth was dry.

Alberto: "Ma... Malina!"

Malina stopped and turned. She looked at Xitl and Tlaxca. They hear another cry.

Tlaxca pointed in a certain direction. Malina hurriedly ran toward the cries. She went from door to door shouting Alberto's name. Finally, she heard a loud pounding coming from the door directly in front of her.

Malina: "Alberto?"

Alberto: "Malina! Malina! I'm here!"

Malina tried to open the door but could not.

Alberto: "There's no key!"

Xitl tried to cut through the iron chains with a small hatchet to no avail.

Malina: "We need Don Gali!"

Xitl: "I'll go get him!"

Gali: "Did someone call?"

The bearded wizard appeared suddenly as if he were there all along! Malina gasped in shock.

Malina: "Gali? Thank God."

Gali smiled.

Gali: "As we should always, your majesty."

Malina smiled peacefully.

Gali: "Stand aside if you please, highness."

Malina moved and gave the Don some room. Gali touched the iron cell door. The wizard's hands glowed bright. Malina stared in complete awe. The glowing light disappeared. Gali pushed the door in. The chains fell off the slit of the door and dropped to the floor. Malina quickly went inside the cell and embraced Alberto. Alberto hugged Malina tightly. Alberto sighed heavily.

Alberto: "Malinali, is it really you?"

Malina: "Yes, my love. It's me!"

Alberto looked deeply into Malina's eyes. He slowly went to kiss her, but fell to the floor. Malina knelt down and put Alberto's head on her lap.

Malina: "Alberto?"

Gali: "Give him water."

Damian knelt down and slowly gave Alberto water to drink from the water pouch bag.

Gali: "Drink slowly."

Alberto drank calmly. He gave a sigh of relief and looked up at the wizard.

Alberto: "Don Gali? I have heard much about you through the years. It's an honor to finally meet you. Thank you for helping me."

Gali: "And I have heard of you, young man. You are most welcome."

Alberto: "The prisoners, they have no food or water. Can you help them?"

Gali: "I will do what I can. The rest is up to the Lord himself, but they cannot come with us. You do understand?"

Alberto: "I understand and thank you."

Gali bowed his head.

Gali: "We must leave. Enrique, Damian, help him."

They helped Alberto down the stairs and out into the open, away from the cathedral prison. Once outside, Malina gave Alberto something to eat. She gave him more water to strengthen him. She was happy to be reunited with him after a whole year. Gali used his powers to release all the prisoners captured by the Emirs. Once freed, Damian and Enrique brought them food. Gali sent them to buy baskets of bread and fish within the village. They also bought a large jar of water to drink. The men were very grateful. Alberto told Gali of the intentions of the Emirs, leaving them behind to starve. Gali felt compassion for the men. However, the idea to take every single man along with them was not an option, not during the middle of a war. His first priority was the safety of the Queen of Hispana, Malina. He had to get her back to the kingdom safely. Once home, then he could return with aid to help the men but not before, not now. He arranged lodgings for the men at the local village tavern close by, at least until they regained their strength.

It was time to journey back. Gali led everyone back across the grassy plain and through the rough lands of the Paz Valley. Almost an entire day passed. Malina noticed something from afar. A lone rider at a distance.

Malina: "Gali? Look."

Gali looked at the far silhouetted figure coming towards them.

Alberto: "Is there danger?"

Gali: "I don't think so."

The horseman came closer and closer. To their surprise, the rider fell off his horse.

Alberto: "Stay here, my love."

Malina: "Alberto?"

Alberto: "It's alright."

Alberto ran to the fallen man. He turned him over and noticed an arrow stuck in his chest. The man gasped for air.

Alberto: "Sir, who are you? Where did you come from?"

The man looked up at Alberto. He struggled as he tried to speak.

"Ugh... I..."

Alberto stared him silently.

"I'm R... Roderic, son of Theodefred."

Alberto: "Roderic?"

Roderic: "King of the Goths."

Alberto recognized the name. Although not officially an elected or crowned king, Roderic gave himself the title only because there were no longer other people of royal blood in his province which was once governed also by his father before him, himself a son of King Chindaswinth of the Goths. Certain beliefs and ways of Roderic never set well with his opposers who always suspected that he usurped power away from Wittiza the rightful king, whom according to legend was the younger brother of King Theodefred and therefore Roderic's uncle. Roderic's opposers accused him of being responsible for Wittiza's assassination and seizing the throne. He was the last lord of his family, with no male heir to continue the 'royal' line. The Goths were nomadic people from Germania who migrated and settled in central and southern Hispana hundreds of years before.

Alberto: "My lord, what happened?"

Roderic: "The Emirs, their army has taken us. Defeated us. My army is no more. All my men are dead."

Gali: "How did you get here?"

Roderic noticed the old wizard above him.

Roderic: "I... I don't know. I rode with no direction. My wife has been taken."

Alberto: "What is her name?"

Roderic: "Egilona, my queen."

Roderic tried to breathe, but could not.

Alberto: "My lord."

Roderic: "We are doomed. Hispana is no more. Run, flee for your lives."

Gali stared boldly at the dying man who was more of a warrior than king.

Alberto: "Gali? Can you help him?"

Gali: "The arrow is too deep. It is hours old, perhaps a day or two. He is beyond my help."

Roderic: "Gali? Don of Vi... Ugh."

Roderic died. Alberto sadly closed his eyes.

Alberto: "He knew of you."

Gali: "And he unknowingly rode deeper into enemy territory. We must flee from enemy territory."

Alberto: "Shouldn't we bury him?"

Gali: "We've no time. Besides, you forget he was a warrior. He'd prefer to be burned instead."

Alberto nodded in agreement. Enrique and Damian covered the warrior king with leaves and tall grass. They lit his body on fire and continued on their journey. By nightfall, they had finally reached the cave from which they came out of. The cave was hidden behind thick brush and shrubs. Tired, they all settled down for the night.

The next day, Malina was awakened by a thundering sound.

Malina: "Gali, what is it?"

Gali: "Shh, listen."

Tlaxca bent down and put his ear down to the ground. He spoke in the native tongue of Nahuatl, the ancient language of the Aztecs. Malina understood. Gali looked at Xitl.

Gali: "What did Tlaxca say?"

Xitl: "My lord, he hears the stampeding of horses, many of them. Coming this way."

Alberto: "Well, it's good we're in here away from sight. Right?"

Suddenly, a loud laughter occurred in the darkness of the cavern. Gali's ring shined its light. Everyone turned in shock as they saw a tall black figure across from them. The Aztec warriors Xitl and Tlaxca guarded Malina.

Malina: "Who is that?"

Gali stared at the approaching figure. He wore a long black cape and wore a long necklace with a small mummified skull.

Gali: "The Zor of Moroc."

Zor: "Very good, wise wizard. It is an honor to finally meet the caretaker of Hispana."

Gali: "I see Endora is not with you, pity."

Zor: "My mistress has no need to be here."

Gali "I dare ask how you found us?"

Zor: "The Witch of Sevi sees everything. You're a wizard. We all have our powers. Some much stronger than others."

The Zor looks at Malina.

Zor: "And who have we here? Highness? It is an honor. And why would the Princess of Aragon be down here in this dreadful and lonely place instead of the glorious and luxurious palace of the kingdom?"

The Zor notices the young Alberto put his arm around Malina and holds her hand with the other. It was obvious.

Zor: "Of course, the greatest reason and motive of all: love."

Gali: "State your business, dark sorcerer."

The Zor stares at Gali.

Zor: "Aside from overtaking your country, I have orders from the Witch of Sevi."

Gali: "And that is?"

The Zor smirks at Malina.

Zor: "To kill the princess!"

Alberto: "Over my dead body!"

The Zor laughs and sighs.

Zor: "That can be easily arranged, my friend."

Alberto charged at the Zor. Gali stopped him.

Gali: "Don't be a fool! You're no match for him!"

Alberto: "I don't care!"

Gali: "Alberto, listen to me! Take Malina out of here. Xitl, Tlaxca, go with them."

Damian: "We stay with you, my lord Gali."

Gali: "No Damian, you and Enrique must go also and protect the queen. No matter what you hear, do not come back."

Malina: "Gali, please."

Gali: "The time has come majesty to protect you and the nation once and for all against this dark foe. If I fail, then I am ever sorry."

Tears ran down Malina's face.

Gali: "It has been an honor my princess, my queen."

Gali bowed his head and motioned Alberto to take her. Everyone else followed. They did not know what to do. There was no other way to go except through the underground cavern which was now blocked by the evil Zor of Moroc. Gali would have to battle the dark sorcerer to get through once again. Once out of the cave, Alberto and Malina look up and are horrified at what they see. Hundreds if not thousands of Emir horsemen line across the high hills looking down at them. Malina cries in deep sorrow. Alberto holds her tight. Damian and Enrique stare in shock and disbelief. All around them are an entire army of Saracens and Emir warriors. Xitl and Tlaxca look at each other. A look of great honor upon them as warriors in time of need for each other's bravery and skills. Xitl looks up and notices the rocky plateaus.

Xitl: "My queen, Alberto, try to make for the plateaus. Their horses cannot step well there. We'll hold them off as long as we can."

Malina: "Xitl, No."

Xitl smiled at his queen and more importantly, his friend. He and Tlaxca kneeled down.

Xitl: "Do not fret my queen. For this purpose, I was born, a great honor I would not dare miss."

Malina: "Xitl, my dear friend. Thank you for everything."

Xitl bowed his head. Malina looked at Tlaxca. She spoke to him in Nahuatl.

Malina: ["Tlaxca? You've always served my house well and I thank you deeply."]

Tlaxca bowed his head in respect to his queen. Alberto looked at Xitl and Tlaxca and then at Damian and Enrique.

Alberto: "Thank you all for helping me, even for a little more time to live. It was not in vain. Thank you."

Xitl bowed his head.

Xitl: "Go."

Alberto looked at Xitl. He and Malina start for the rocky plateaus.

Xitl: "Well my friends? It seems we have a battle to fight. We still have our glass shields Don Gali gave us. Let's use them wisely."

Enrique: "And I have some clear dust. We've already seen how effective it worked against the Sogs."

Xitl: "Yes, very effective. We'll wait for them to get closer before we use it."

Damian: "It's been an honor, my friend."

Xitl: "The honor is mine Damian and Enrique."

Xitl and Tlaxca walk down deeper into the valley. They see the army is still far off. They start their traditional Aztec battle chants and ceremonial war cries. The Saracens slowly ride down the hills. Xitl and Tlaxca dance around and around in a circle. Damian and Enrique draw their swords in readiness, not knowing how the outcome would be.

Gali and the Zor of Moroc stare at each other. The Zor looks up at the caverns and bolts of lasers fire out of his eyes, hitting the solid boulders causing them to break into great pieces of falling rocks, covering the opening to the cave. Gali looks in astonishment. The Zor grins.

Zor: "To keep your friends from getting back in."

They slowly move around in a circular motion. The Zor pushes his hands through the air, sending the old wizard backward. The Don falls onto the rocks of the ground. The Zor laughs. Gali tries to get up. The Zor swiftly pierces his magical hands at Gali, once again raising him into the air and tossing him onto the hard ground.

Zor: "Much too easy!"

From the ground, Gali pushes his mighty hand into the Zor making the dark sorcerer fly backward and hitting a rock solid wall. Gali rises to his feet as does the Zor. The two gaze into each other's eyes. Bright lasers shoot out of the Zor's eyes and fire at Gali. Gali stops the beams by crossing his wrists, protected by his metallic vambrace armbands. The Zor raises his hand in the air and thrusts his fingers toward Gali, creating a heavy force pushing against the old bearded wizard. Gali tries his best to resist the mighty Zor's awesome power.

Zor: "You're past getting old wizard. You are old! You are no match for the likes of me. My powers are beyond you."

Gali continues to resist the strength of the dark force.

Zor: "It's over wizard! Admit defeat!"

Gali: "You... talk too much!"

Gali broke through the dark force and struck the Zor hard across the face and kicked him. The Zor fell. Gali's magical hands raised the Zor up high and dropped him hard to the ground. Gali again lifted the evil sorcerer and again dropped him down, slamming the mighty Zor hard. Gali sighed and caught his breath for a moment. Suddenly, a long wire whip lashed out at Gali's feet tripping him hard on his back. The Zor angrily whipped at the Don over and over again. The ferocious lashes cut the wizard's hands and face, ripping his hooded cloak to shreds. The Zor laughed loudly.

Zor: "Do you surrender? Do you surrender?"

Gali pushed his hand at the Zor with all his might in midair. The Zor dropped his whip and caught hold of his throat. Gali was choking him without actually touching him. The Zor dropped to his knees gasping for air. Gali struggled to his feet. The Zor continued choking. Gali looked at the dark sorcerer. Holding his throat with one hand, the Zor pierced his other hand strongly, sending a sharp razor pain into Gali's side. The Don of Villalobos screamed in terrible agony. The pain was unbearable, but the old wizard did not let go of his mystical grip. The Zor struggled and struggled for air but could not. The Zor of Moroc fell dead to the ground. Gali then fell to his knees. A great amount of power was drained from him.

The first group of Saracens galloped toward Xitl and Tlaxca. Xitl threw his long spear. The traveling spear found its sheath in a Saracen rider. The warrior fell off his horse. Tlaxca threw his deadly atlatl. The long, wooden arrow-like spear plunges deep into an Emir warrior. They are soon surrounded by oncoming riders. The rest of the army remained on the hill looking down. They were in no hurry. After throwing all their spears, the two Aztec warriors were now ready for close range combat. Horseman after horseman charged at them with everything they had. Using their magical shields Gali gave them, Xitl and Tlaxca blocked off every arrow and spear thrown at them. They in turn used the maqua-huitl or 'macana', long clubs with sharp obsidian rock edges embedded within the wooden frame. They sliced the horse's legs, cutting them as they galloped toward them. They did it regrettably, they hated having to harm the beautiful horses. The fallen horsemen rose to their feet and drew their swords. Xitl was no fool. He knew full well his wooden club was no match against steel, so he relied simply upon his fighting skills, agility, ability, and speed. They served him well. The two Aztecs were back to back. They stepped forward and fought and immediately returned with their backs facing each other.

Damian and Enrique fought hard with their sword and shield. The two apprentices also used the power Gali taught them effectively by forcing oncoming horsemen to fall off against their own will simply by waving their hands toward them. As the army drew closer, the two young would-be wizards used the magical clear dust to their advantage. They blew the dust from their hands. The magic dust independently became as if alive and found its way right into the eyes of the Saracen and Emir army. The warriors screamed in pain. They could no longer see. But the enemy warriors also had their own wizards and sorcerers. The dark wizards waved their hands and their staffs sending the two apprentices into the air. They both landed hard on the ground.

Enrique: "They're too strong! Back to the cave!"

Xitl: "The cave is blocked! We can't get in! Besides, I would never go back without my queen!"

Enrique: "Nor I!"

Xitl smiled.

Xitl: "My kind of warrior!"

Enrique: "How can you smile at a time like this?"

Xitl shrugged his shoulders.

Xitl: "An eagle knight knows no fear."

Xitl points to Tlaxca.

Xitl: "And neither does a jaguar knight!"

Xitl, Tlaxca, Damian, and Enrique gathered together, back to back, with their long magical glass shields protecting them. The army closed in on them. All four friends looked at each other.

Xitl: "This is it my friends. You fought well, remember that."

Malina and Alberto climbed their way up the rocky plateaus. They hid behind a large boulder. Malina wept for her friends.

Alberto: "I'm sorry Malina, but there is nothing we can do. Remember their bravery."

Malina laid next to Alberto. Alberto sighed.

Alberto: "The Great War is finally upon us."

Malina looked at Alberto.

Alberto: "We cannot survive. We cannot escape."

Alberto looked at Malina sadly.

Alberto: "You saved me, even if for a while. You saved me, my love. Thank you."

Malina: "You're welcome."

Alberto's eyes watered.

Alberto: "I'm sorry I can't save you. I..."

Malina: "Shh."

Malina kissed Alberto.

Malina: "You make me happy and I love you Alberto. I'm happy to spend my last moments with you. I have no regrets."

Alberto hugged his queen and cried. Malina wiped away his tears and kissed him softly. She rose up and stood before her beloved knight. Alberto looked at his love. Malina slowly bared her shoulders. She pulled her gown down, exposing her breasts.

Alberto: "Malina?"

Malina took off her entire gown. She walked toward Alberto naked.

Alberto: "We can't."

Malina: "I want you to take me. Here. Now."

Alberto: "Malina, I..."

Malina: "Take me before they do."

Alberto stared at his beautiful queen.

Alberto: "Malina."

Malina: "You said it yourself, we're not going to live. We'll be dead before tomorrow. You know what they'll do to me after they kill you."

Alberto closed his eyes in sorrow. He knew she was right. Malina gently touched Alberto's face and looked at him.

Malina: "If anything, I want you to be the first."

Alberto looked down sadly.

Alberto: "My love. I'm... I'm filthy. I..."

Malina: "I don't care, Alberto. I don't care."

They both looked deep into each other's eyes. Alberto slowly aimed for Malina's lips. They kissed passionately. Alberto undressed himself. The two made love laying on top of their clothing. Alberto took his beloved Malina. Malina made love to her beloved knight Alberto. It was a special and important moment for them both. Afterward, Malina opened her eyes and sighed. She whispered to herself softly as Alberto slept.

Malina: {"This is love....this is love."}

Alberto slowly opened his eyes. He looks around. Malina is nowhere to be found! He looks over the ledge of the plateau. He sees Malina far down below, walking across the valley. Alberto shouts from afar. Malina hears him, but pays no mind. As far as she's concerned the end is upon them. There is no escape from their fate. Everyone, all her escorts, entourage, and friends are dead. Alberto quickly tries to put on his clothes. Malina keeps walking. She comes face to face with the Saracen leader.

Saracen: "Greetings! You must be Princess Malina? I've heard of you."

Malina: "I'm flattered."

Saracen: "Where is your gentleman?"

Malina: "Why do you ask?"

Saracen: "Give him to us and you may go in peace."

Malina: "I'm not a fool Saracen, I know you'll kill me also. Why should you let me go?"

The Saracen leader laughs.

Saracen: "I'm a reasonable man. No need for me to kill you, the elements alone can do that. We'll leave you here to die in the burning valley."

Malina looks at the Saracen rider.

Saracen: "I know where he is, on top of the high plateau. Me and my men can outwait him. He cannot stay up there forever. Sooner or later, he will come down and we will be waiting for him. Give him to me peacefully and I promise to hasten his death. Refuse and he will die in extreme agony."

Malina looks up into heaven and closes her eyes. She prays softly. The Saracen laughs.

Saracen: "What is your answer highness?"

Malina looks at him boldly.

Malina: "I'll never give him to you. You'll have to kill me first."

Saracen: "HA, HA, HA! Defiant to the end, I like that. Your god has abandoned you my princess. Your land is now ours. All lands will be ours. We will conquer the world. We will die for the faith and the faith will be died for. Innocent blood will be shed and there will be many who'll perish. Death is upon you, whether by our hand or by yours. You can stay on that mountain. Within a few days, you'll be dead. You are without hope."

'Without hope,' Malina could not accept those words. The only thing she had left was her faith.

Malina: "You can conquer the lands, You can conquer the people, but you can never ever conquer my God."

Saracen: "Ah, yes, the carpenter. The workman who died for the sins of the world. The promised one who gave up his life so that all men can have hope of salvation and avoid eternal damnation in burning everlasting hell."

Malina just stared at the Saracen commander.

Saracen: "Oh yes, my princess, I know of your god and I do not believe any of it. False! All false! None of it is true. Your god is not god! We are the sons of the true faith! Only the 'One' is god! Now kneel and surrender."

Malina: "Only Christ is God. I will not kneel to your false god and I will never surrender."

The Saracen warrior laughs.

Saracen: "Do you think your carpenter will deliver you from my hand?"

Malina: "I am already delivered."

The Saracen looked angrily at Malina.

Saracen: "As you wish."

The Saracen rides back to his men. The rest of the entire Saracen and Emir army stood high upon the hills. The Saracen leader approaches his men.

Saracen: "Our princess is not only stubborn but brave. No matter, they are both vanquished. Run her down, trample her deep into the earth!"

The army advanced. Malina looked back at the high rocky plateau. She saw Alberto running toward her from far away.

Alberto: "Malina! Malina, NO!"

Malina: {"I love you."}

The army of black dressed riders came charging heavily on the ground stampeding toward Malina. Malina looked at them. She closed her eyes. She started walking forward toward the coming army of horsemen. How brave she was standing in the middle of certain death.

Alberto: "Malina!"

Malina stared at the stampeding horde.

Malina: "My faith will not waiver."

The thundering of hooves got closer and closer! Malina gasped heavily. The ground shook as if an earthquake erupted! She closed her eyes.

Malina: {"Lord."}

The Saracen and Emir army draw their broadswords and yell loudly.

"AAHHH!!!"

Suddenly, fire from heaven shot down between Malina and the deadly charging army! The great fire exploded the ground! Riders fell from their horses left and right. Some were engulfed in flames. Malina looks up at the beautiful blue sky.

Malina: "Milagro!"

Milagro: ["You...(puff) ...called me my princess? (puff)"]

Malina was overjoyed! The Spanish dragon swooped down and Malina quickly climbed on its back.

Malina: "Oh Milagro, I've missed you!"

Milagro smiled, baring his white razor teeth and long fang-like tusks.

Milagro: ["I've... (puff) I've missed you too highness!"]

Malina: "Where's Antonio?"

Antonio: ["At your service my princess!"]

Malina smiled.

Malina: "Antonio!"

Antonio smiled at Malina. Behind Antonio were his friends and allies the Dynos! Several three-horned Triceratops and sharp-tailed Stegosaurus came charging at the enemy. Flying Pteranodons terrorized the fleeing army.

Milagro: ["Hang on tight! (puff)"]

Saracen: "Archers!"

The archers shot arrows at the two giant dragons, but they did not penetrate due to the dragon's thick hard scales. Milagro flew Malina away from danger.

Malina: "We have to save Alberto! He's down there!"

Antonio flew above the Saracens and Emirs. He breathed fire down onto them, scattering the entire army. Many ran for their lives. They were no match at all for this deadly dragon! Alberto could not believe his eyes when he saw a great gigantic beast hovering over him.

Malina: "Alberto! It's alright!"

Alberto: "Malina?"

Malina: "Yes! Come on!"

Alberto climbed on Milagro's neck and onto his back. Malina held onto Alberto tight.

Malina: "Milagro?"

Milagro: ["Yes highness? (puff)"]

Malina: "What about Gali? Xitl...?"

Alberto: "Malina. We must leave."

Milagro: ["I must get you home highness."]

Malina nodded her head sadly. Milagro flapped his long, extended bat-like wings and flew high into the air. The huge dragon soared back to the kingdom of Hispana. Days later, the war was finally over. The Dyno allies had helped achieve a great victory over the Moranic barbarians. The Northen army of Hispana crushed the evil Emirs. At last it was over, the time for celebration was at hand, a celebration of peace, a celebration of the coronation. Princess Malina was finally and officially going to be crowned Queen of Hispana! All the people came to see the event.

Malina was in her private room getting ready. Her maidservants helped her with her beautiful white gown. Lila the Arielantis fairy hovered in the air toward Malina.

Lila: "Your majesty? Someone is here to see you."

Malina: "Oh, thank you Lila. I'll be right out."

Lila: "Yes highness."

Lila flew through and vanished through the door. Malina checked herself in the long mirror. She thanked her maidservants and went out the door. Malina saw someone standing with a hooded cloak draped over.

Malina: "Yes? May I help you?"

Stranger: "No invitation this time to your very own coronation, highness?"

Malina paused. She recognized the voice. Could it be? It had to!

Malina: "Gali?"

The stranger flipped back his hood and smiled at the would-be queen!

Gali: "Greetings your majesty!"

Malina: "Gali! Oh, thank you Lord Jesus! Thank you!"

Malina ran and hugged her dear friend.

Gali: "Ha, ha, ha!"

Malina: "But... how? Wha..."

Gali: "Shh."

Gali turned and waved. Four other persons came and stood before the princess.

Malina's jaw dropped in complete awe.

Malina: "Xitl! Tlaxca! Damian! Enrique!"

All four smiled at Malina. They kneeled before her.

Malina: "No! No! My friends will not kneel today, not today."

Malina embraced her friends. She wept happily.

Malina: "Oh Xitl! I'm so happy you're alive."

Xitl: "Me too highness! Me too! I am so glad. I feared I would never see you again."

Malina turned to Gali.

Malina: "Gali? What happened? I thought all of you were... gone."

Gali: "For a moment, so did I. After I battled with the Zor of Moroc, I was completely drained. I almost died. The Zor was my greatest adversary ever. Anyhow, after I came to, I managed enough power to remove the huge rocks covering the entrance to the cave. I helped our four warriors fight off the enemy and then something strange happened."

Malina: "What? What?"

Gali: "We disappeared."

Malina: "Disappeared? You mean you all vanished into thin air?"

Gali: "For the most part, yes. It seems the magical shields I created took on a life of their own. At first, the enemy enclosed the four. Nothing happened. But when I was among them, it was different. When the enemy surrounded us again, we all stood back to back once more. And that's when the shields gave a bright glowing light and then we were gone. But I'm afraid I can't take all the credit. Enrique is the real savior."

Malina: "Enrique?'

Gali: "Enrique, explain."

Enrique: "Well your majesty, the night we spent in the cave after we saved Alberto, I awoke and decided to check on our equipment. In doing so, I accidently spilled my bag of clear dust. I was stunned when I saw the clear dust making its way, sprinkling itself onto my glass shield. I was very impressed! It was like a magnetic force. I thought why not? So, therefore I decided to sprinkle clear dust on the rest of the shields for extra protection, I guess. I know it was silly of me. My guess is Don Gali, being the creator of the magical dust, well, the dust somehow became drawn to his person when he got close to us as we carried the sprinkled shields and so we disappeared."

Malina: "And where did you find yourselves?"

Gali: "Funny enough, we awoke and found ourselves in my temple in the Pyr mountain region."

Malina: "Enrique? Your actions saved all of you, thank you."

Gali: "I was worried about you and Alberto. There was no way to get back to you. However, you're here, safe and sound."

Malina: "Thanks to Antonio and Milagro, they arrived just in time."

Gali: "My trustworthy and reliable behemoths. I told you you'd see them again."

Malina: "Yes, you did."

Gali: "Anyway, thanks to Enrique's mishap, we all survived long enough to tell and laugh about it. Now I must figure out how to go back and forth, disappear and reappear with this new magical discovery of my young apprentice."

Damian: "And without passing out and having to wake up!"

Gali: "Exactly Damian! We were lucky."

Malina: "Lucky? Hmm, I don't know about that."

Gali: "Oh?"

Malina: "I did pray at times. I'd like to think my prayers were answered by the Most High."

Gali: "I think you're right. God does work in mysterious ways indeed."

Malina looked at Gali.

Malina: "I'm happy you're here. I love you Gali. Thank you."

Gali: "And I love you too highness."

Malina hugged Gali and smiled happily.

Gali: "Well, my goodness! Here we are talking and boasting about ourselves and you have a coronation to attend!"

Malina laughed joyfully. Just then an official guard came forth and told Malina it was time. Malina looked at her friends. She was so very grateful they were here with her. They all bowed their heads in respect. Malina entered the royal hall. All the officials and dignitaries were present. Governors of other provinces were also there to witness the coronation. Malina slowly stepped up the royal stairs and sat on the throne that was once her father's. A royal bishop walked toward Malina with the jeweled crown in his hands. He raised it up and gently placed it upon Malina's head.

Royal Bishop: "HAIL, QUEEN MALINA! HAIL TO THE QUEEN OF HISPANA!"

["HAIL, QUEEN Malina! HAIL TO THE QUEEN OF HISPANA!"]

Royal Bishop: "Majesty, stand and be recognized."

Malina stood up calmly and smiled at the crowd. Everyone cheered the new queen.

Malina opened a scroll and read her first order aloud.

Malina: "My first order as Queen of Hispana! Concerning Sonia Hernandez, you all know the claims she made about my father, King Esteban I. Whether true or false, I hereby banish her from the realm! She is never to return! Concerning Simona Hernandez, the matter is still being investigated. However, I do believe she is my father's daughter and is not at fault in this scandal. Therefore, as Queen of Hispana, I declare my half-sister Simona Hernandez, Princess of Navarre! I welcome my sister into the royal family! Thus, may the matter be closed forever!"

Everyone cheered. Malina rolled the scroll and gave it to a royal servant. Alberto stepped forward and took Malina's hand. He gently led her down the steps and down the red carpet. A young girl walked toward Queen Malina and kneeled before her in tears. Malina looked at her with compassion.

Malina: "Arise Princess Simona, no need for tears."

Simona: "Your majesty, I'm so sorry. Please forgive me."

Malina: "There is nothing to forgive, my sister."

Simona looked at Malina.

Simona: "I promise to do good always. Thank you Malina. Thank you."

Malina embraced her sister and kissed her.

Malina: "So, are we still on for our long walks by the lakes and picnics by the trees?"

Simona smiled happily.

Simona: "Yes! Yes my sister, yes!"

The two sisters hugged again happily. Simona looked at Alberto. She whispered in Malina's ear.

Simona: {"He's handsome!"}

Malina: {"I know! Isn't he a dream?"}

Simona kissed her sister. Suddenly, the palace announcer pounded the floor with his long decorated spear.

Palace Announcer: "THE QUEEN MOTHER! HER MAJESTY, Queen Omeya!"

Malina gasped. She could not believe her mother was finally home! She looked on as Queen Omeya walked toward her with an entire noble entourage of both Aztec eagle warriors and jaguar knights following close behind. The Queen Mother's decorated crown was adorned with long bright Quetzal feathers. She wore a brightly colored gown with a long silver cape. Queen Omeya looked at her daughter proudly. Malina smiled and hugged her mother.

Malina: "Mama! I'm happy you're home. I've missed you so much."

Queen Omeya: "And I've missed you Malinali. I come home to find my princess is now Queen of Hispana."

Malina smiled.

Malina: "Mama? Father..."

Queen Omeya: "I know daughter, I know."

Malina looked down sadly.

Queen Omeya: "This is your day Malinali, a day of happiness. No room for sorrow."

Malina: "Thank you Mama."

Queen Omeya looked at Alberto and smiled.

Malina: "Mama, this is Alberto."

Queen Omeya: "I remember. Greetings, young knight."

Alberto kissed the Queen Mother's hand.

Alberto: "It is an honor, your majesty."

Queen Omeya: "And now my lovely daughter, go and present yourself to the people of Hispana."

Malina: "Yes, your majesty."

Queen Malina of Hispana continued forward. Alberto was dressed in his knight's attire, donning a long royal red cape with gold embroidered edges. The two walked outside of the royal hall and out of the castle so that all the people could see the new queen. Guards were present everywhere. They wore shiny breastplates and beautiful morion helmets with colorful plumage dangling. Even the great jaguar and eagle knights were present. In celebration and in honor to the queen, the jaguar knights released beautiful Quetzal birds into the air. The flying Quetzals exploded with colors as they flew above the San Juan castle! Their long tail-feather train followed them. Malina could not believe how beautiful they were. The Aztecs gave a ceremonial dance. The crowds cheered happily. All the people were at ease. The kingdom was at peace!

Malina looked at her handsome knight. Alberto stared at his gorgeous queen.

Malina: "Caballero?"

Alberto: "My lady?"

Malina: "Didn't you once ask for my hand in marriage?"

Alberto looked at Malina.

Alberto: "I did, my lady."

Malina: "I think I'll take you up on that offer."

Alberto: "Really?"

Malina: "Oh yes!"

Alberto: "So you would dare marry someone like me?"

Malina: "I would. What say you knight?"

Alberto smiled.

Alberto: "I do."

Malina put her arms around Alberto.

Malina: "Come here 'man of God'!"

Alberto and Malina kissed each other lovingly, sealing their engagement.

["ANYONE WANT A RIDE? (puff)"]

Malina turned and smiled. Her two giant dragons stood before her. Alberto smiled.

Malina: "Aww Milagro."

Milagro lowered his giant head. Malina patted him softly. Alberto patted Antonio happily.

Alberto: "Our dear friends."

Malina looked at Alberto.

Malina: "Well, my handsome knight? Shall we take flight and enjoy the scenery of the kingdom from above?"

Alberto: "Yes, my queen. Let us take flight!"

Malina laughed happily. Antonio and Milagro flew up and away, soaring above the beautiful kingdom.

In the coming days, the knight and his queen were finally married. And they would live happily ever after in the castle of San Juan!

Deep in the caverns of the Atlas Mountains, loud moaning and groaning are all around. Howling can be heard from afar. Loud screams echo throughout the vast blackness. Large rats run around squeaking. Glowing eyes pierce out of the darkness. In the shadows, a dark figure slowly walks toward a river. She kneels down and dips her frail and bony hand into the red river of blood! She looks deep into the bloody waters.

Witch of Sevi: "You may have won this time my Mexican princess! But there will be another time! I, Endora, shall return! HA, HA, HA, HA, HA, HA, HA, HA, HA, HA, HA...!"

The old woman rises and steps away. She continues onward and disappears into the darkness.

The End